THE
TRUE KING

Book 2 of Fall to Darkness

to Ron Lynn –
enjoy this adventure!
Summer Sullivan

SUMMER SULLIVAN

SUMMER SULLIVAN
Published by AuSable Publishing
Ausablepublishing.com

Printed in the United States of America
First Printing 2022
First Edition 2022

ISBN: 978-1-7373611-4-5

To LeMay and Rem, the first to explore the world of Fall to Darkness

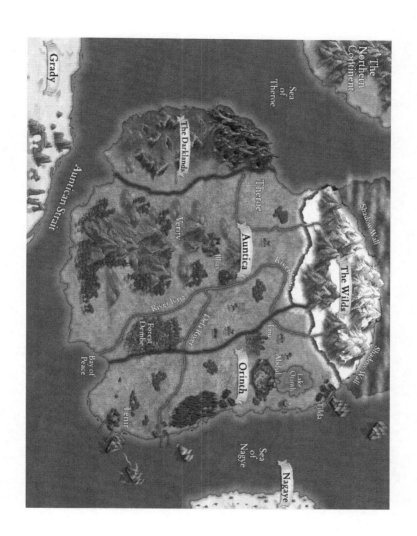

PART II

Prologue

"**I** *wish you would stay, dear."*

The boy sat across from the plump old woman, his hands clutching a cup of tea that she had made him. He wanted to tell her desperately that he hated tea. But he had been pretending to like it, for her sake, since he was seven years old. He wasn't going to stop now. He took another swallow of the terrible drink and managed to choke it down without giving away the truth.

Lola, the woman who had basically raised him, was a kind woman, slightly overweight, with grey hair and wrinkled skin. The boy couldn't remember her ever looking any different. She had always been like that. She wore a floral dress that was faded and grasped her own cup of tea as she sat opposite him behind her desk. In front of her were biscuits and honey, a delicacy he knew she only reserved for special occasions. And the boy visiting the orphanage was, apparently, a special occasion.

"Me too, Lola. But you know I can't," he said, reaching for a biscuit. He felt slightly impolite. It was the third one he had taken in the time they had been sitting down. The boy wasn't being greedy; it just happened to be the first time he had eaten something substantial in nearly a week.

Lola sighed, watching as he slathered the biscuit in honey. "It's not the same without you here. And I hate the thought of you being on the streets all by yourself, not eating, having to steal to survive. You might get hurt, or worse."

She was right, alarmingly so, but he still wouldn't change his mind. "I know, Lola. I'll be okay. I promise I will be. But you know it's just as bad for me here as it is on the streets."

Lola looked down, sighing. "I'm so sorry. I wish there was something I could do to make it better. You know how hard I've tried to get those boys to stop, they just..."

her voice trailed off as her bottom lip started to quiver. Lola had secretly always been an emotional being who often broke down in front of the boy. She would never allow the other children to see her like this, but he was an exception.

"It's not your fault, Lola. Like you said, there's nothing you can do. Don't worry about me. I can take care of myself. As long as I can keep coming back here every once in a while and see you, that's fine with me." He took a bite of his biscuit and gave her a smile.

She laughed, though tears had started to well up in her eyes. "You only come back for the biscuits."

"That's not true!" He pretended to ponder for a moment. "Okay, maybe they are part of the reason." He shot her a grin.

Lola wiped a tear away before it could fall down her cheek. "You always have a place here, dear. I know you haven't had the best childhood, but I did the best I could. You're a boy who has been plagued with darkness you don't deserve. But you handle it well."

Lola had always said things to him, throughout his childhood, about the darkness he possessed. The boy didn't understand it. Yes, he had his own form of darkness, but didn't everyone at the orphanage? None of them had parents or families who wanted them. Most of them weren't educated and didn't even know how to read. Lola tried her best, but what could one woman do among almost fifty children? Yes, he had darkness, but it was impossible not to. It wasn't just him.

But he didn't say that to Lola.

He opened his mouth to respond when he heard the laughter outside the door. The boy hesitated, waiting for it to pass, before he spoke, "I should probably get going, Lola, before they know I'm here."

She sighed again and the boy suddenly wished that he could make things better for her, this woman that had given her life to children. She could have had a husband and family of her own. He hoped that she felt like they were her family. The boys at the orphanage could be ruthless, and they were, but no one ever hurt Lola.

They hurt him though.

"Yes, you must go. Take the rest of the biscuits in your bag," she said and the boy grinned as he stuffed the three remaining into his pack. It held everything he owned, which wasn't much: a single change of clothing, a small knife, and now, some biscuits, as well as a small drawstring bag of money that he had managed to take from the boys.

He shouldn't steal. He knew stealing was wrong but then again, he had nothing. These boys still had the orphanage, but they had chased him away from it. The least he deserved was their money. It was enough to buy him meals for the next week as he *floated from alley to rooftop, wherever there was a warm corner for him to sleep in. Plus, if he saved enough of it, he might be able to purchase a blanket, which would be the most incredible asset.*

"Thank you, Lola. For everything."

She tried to smile, but it came out as a grimace. "You're just thanking me for the biscuits, aren't you?"

He gave a sad smile in return. "No. I'm thanking you for you."

Lola wiped another tear off her cheek and reached across the desk, squeezing his hand once. "Stay safe, you hear? I should expect to see you again soon."

He squeezed it back. "I will. I'll see you soon."

And as he turned around to leave, the boy got the strangest feeling that he wouldn't. He tried to shake off the sensation, waving at Lola one more time before he left her office, but it wouldn't go away. Why wouldn't he see her again? He had been living on the streets for almost a year now and had managed to see her at least once a month, sometimes more. Why wouldn't he continue that?

He managed to escape the rest of the building without running into the boys who had made it a habit to torment him his entire childhood, the reason he had left in the first place. He exited onto the busy street, taking a deep breath of the salty air, trying to decide where he would go now. He had money for a real dinner, which was an improvement, but he was full of the biscuits. He wouldn't eat until he absolutely had to. Until then, he could go to the market and try to pickpocket some of the tourists. Maybe he could go by the harbor and watch the ships come in instead, because seeing Lola made him feel slightly guilty about his stealing. Maybe he could go find an adequate rooftop to camp out on that night. The possibilities were endless.

Any future plans disappeared from his mind as he locked eyes with the boy that hated him the most. He was twenty feet away from him, in a large group of the others. They were approaching the orphanage, but they had stopped as they saw the boy. No. He thought he had heard them go by Lola's office, heard them go upstairs. There was no way they were seeing him now, after he had stolen from every single one of their rooms.

The boy at the front of the gang smiled at him.

He didn't wait to see what would happen as he bolted in the other direction, pumping his arms as hard as he could, weaving between the people walking the opposite way. He didn't even have to look back to know that the boys were running after him.

The boy knew the streets well. He had memorized every back alley, every shortcut, every path that existed in Tenir, and it was a big city. He used all of them as he made his escape, stumbling forward with everything he had because if they reached him, he knew he was dead. These were the boys who had made his childhood a nightmare and wanted to continue it. He gasped for breath with every turned corner, every rushed apology as he ran someone over.

It was for nothing. The boys knew the streets as well as he did, possibly better. They had all grown up on them, and as the boy looked back, he saw they were no further away than they had been before.

He was running out of energy. He gripped the straps of his bag tightly as he turned another corner.

And ran straight into a dead end.

He froze as his eyes fell on the brick wall that was in front of him.

He had taken the wrong turn. He wanted an alley that cut to another street and instead, he had gotten a dead end.

The boy turned around, but it was too late. They had reached him.

He counted about six or seven of them as he backed into the brick wall. He recognized each of their faces, but most of the names escaped him except one: the leader, the same one who had always been the leader, the one who hated him the most, Conli. He was a few years older than the boy, with bright blonde hair and dark eyes. His skin was pasty, and he had always looked like a rat to the boy.

"You come crawling back again," Conli laughed wickedly. "I'm not surprised in the least. You can't stay away from Lola, can you? Let me ask you something…"

"Don't you dare," the boy said breathlessly. His backpack was on his back and it would take too much time to dig his knife out. There was no chance of outrunning them, they blocked his only exit like a wall. The brick around him was too tall and too steep to climb. There were no options.

He might die.

The boy wasn't ready to die.

He was fourteen years old, for gods' sake.

The rest of the boys laughed. "Oh man, you never get old, you know that?" Conli continued, starting to walk towards him. "Tell us, what exactly do you do when you come back to grace us with your presence? You left and I thought that was the last I'd have to see of you. But it seems that every time you come around, I lose my money, my hard-earned money. Do you know anything about that?" Conli asked, stopping only feet from him as the rest of the boys followed.

The boy shrugged. "I couldn't tell you, Conli."

Conli paced in front of him as the boy tensed, just waiting for the strike. He could hold his own in a fight, but seven against one? He had no chance. "So you don't know anything about how our money keeps mysteriously disappearing?"

"Not a clue, Conli. I don't live there anymore. Why don't you ask Hans where the money went? I heard he has to pay to get any woman."

Hans, a large boy with bright red hair, growled as he started towards him, but Conli held a hand up. "Don't let him goad you like that, Hans. Isn't this how he always wins? He manages to use his words and stop us, but not this time, boy. We know it's been you who's stealing our money. Just tell us the truth..." he studied his fingernails with a small smile, "and we'll let you go without touching you."

The boy snorted, "Unlikely."

"Come on," Conli laughed. "Just tell us the truth. Isn't that what Lola always says? 'The truth will set you free'. Tell us the truth and we'll let you go. We won't touch you. We'll set you free."

The boy bit his lip. "Conli, I don't have your money. I go to the orphanage to visit Lola. Let me go and I won't come back. I'll leave you alone."

Conli shook his head. "Not good enough. The truth."

The boy took a deep breath. There was no way out of this. He wasn't running and he wasn't fighting back. He felt his heart beating hard in his chest as he realized the truth. He wasn't going to get away this time. Sweat dripped down his forehead and he pinched the skin of his hand to keep it from shaking. Not this time. And he was afraid. He was very afraid.

But he wasn't going down that easy. He wouldn't give his life to them.

"What if I told you that I was stealing your money so I could take your mama out for a night on the town, Conli?" the boy asked him, with a tone of mockery. "Oh, wait. You don't have to worry about that, do you?"

Conli's smile immediately disappeared, replaced by a scowl. "You take that back," he hissed.

"You know, it's good both your parents are dead, Conli. You don't have to see your ugly mama and know it's from her you got your looks."

Conli charged him and the last thing he saw was a flash of his pale skin before his back crashed into the ground.

He didn't even have time to defend himself. A punch to the face, he felt his nose break as he cried out. Conli picked him up by his underarms. He struggled as Conli, who was much larger than him, threw him into the brick wall. His head crashed into the hard surface and he felt the skin scrape and the blood start dripping down. It *didn't matter as he was thrown back onto the ground, getting kicked in the gut three times. He heard a crack and the pain exploded throughout his body.*

"Alright, boys," Conli said, breathing heavily. "Have at him."

Punches, kicks, spit, curses all flung towards him at rapid speed and he took each hit, repeatedly, to every part of his body. He curled into a ball as it continued, over and over again, the pain exploding on each of his nerves. He whimpered softly. It had to stop, but it didn't. Over and over and over again, to his gut, to his face, to his back. Everything he was, was pain, and it wasn't stopping.

He was going to die.

It was a somber thought, but an accurate one.

He had been on the brink more times than he could count, but something about this felt more final. Occasionally, someone would catch him pickpocketing and try to beat him for it, but he had always escaped. Once in a while, he ran into someone on the streets who wasn't exactly friendly and the process repeated itself. But this was different. This was inescapable, like the dead end of the alley he had run into.

And as someone's foot met his gut, he threw up the remaining biscuits.

It wasn't fair, he thought, that I should die without knowing who I am.

He had met his father, maybe five or six times, or at least the man who claimed to be his father. But that man didn't want him, and had left him to grow up at the orphanage. The boy tried not to care. Maybe he had a mother. The boy had begged Lola to tell him. She had been the head of the orphanage since its founding and would've known the mother he had never met. She would've made both of his parents fill out the appropriate paperwork, but he knew that hadn't happened. He had searched her office time and time again and found nothing. He didn't know who he was, spare only his name, and now he was going to die?

No, he thought, no. That wasn't how it was going to end.

The anger overcame him before he even realized what was happening.

He had grown up in an orphanage because his mother and father hadn't wanted him. Because of that, he had endured years of torment from the boys who currently beat him. He had been shoved into a house with other children who were unwanted, and they had endured together. Despite it all, the boy had tried to be a good person. He tried to help Lola when he could, teaching the younger children to read, doing the dishes, setting the table, contributing in any way, and this was how he was repaid for it?

He was deserted at birth and this was the lot the gods had given him?

Well, maybe the gods weren't there. If they were, would they really let this be happening to a fourteen-year-old boy?

And as he heard one of his ribs crack as their feet met it, the tips of their worn-out shoes still managing to inflict pain, he snapped.

For so many years, he had kept the faith, hoping his life would get better if he kept trying. Lola always spoke of manifesting. Manifest goodness and the universe will repay you.

He had tried. He had given everything just to try and be a good person, but they wouldn't let him be.

The boy was done trying to be a good person.

He opened his eyes and the anger exploded within him.

The first person he saw was Conli. As his tormentor looked back down at him, something in his expression changed. The boy wanted him, needed him to feel the pain that he had put the boy through. He closed his eyes and barely managed to lift his hand.

Conli started screaming.

The rest of the boys stumbled back as their leader fell to his knees, shrieking in pain as the boy felt the anger rush through him. He rolled over, still cradling his gut but his eyes were on Conli. Anger at him, anger at his parents who had left him, anger at the world and the gods who allowed such evil. What was the point of it all? People died and children were in orphanages and mothers couldn't feed their children and people slept in alleys at night because they had no home. What was the point of it all and what gods made it possible for it to happen? He felt that anger and unleashed it on Conli.

He had never felt anything like this.

With one eye swollen shut, the boy watched with the other as Conli began foaming at the mouth, shaking so badly that he could hear the cracks of his bones. The screaming hadn't ceased, but the boy could barely hear it over the ringing in his own ears, the mass of anger that had suddenly been awakened.

What was happening?

How was he doing this?

Conli collapsed to the ground, a final scream ringing out. His body convulsed once, then went still.

The boy closed his eyes again.

He had just killed a man.

Somehow.

"Conli?" one of the other boys spoke in a shaking voice.

Conli didn't move.

"*What did you do to him?*" *the voice screamed at the boy.*

He had managed to sit up, his head and entire body throbbing from the pain he had just been put through. He dragged his eyes up to where the group of boys now stood, huddled together in fear, staring at where Conli laid on the ground.

"*Get out of here or I will kill every single one of you,*" *the boy breathed, though it didn't sound like him speaking anymore.*

They didn't think twice. The remaining boys sprinted out of the alley and he was alone.

But not alone. He glanced at the body that was laying only feet away from him. Conli's eyes were still open wide, petrified with fear, but he was dead. His pants were stained with urine and he was starting to reek as the boy tried to stand up, and fell down, too close to the corpse. He squirmed away, and suddenly vomited all over the alley.

He had killed a man.

With his mind.

He had nothing in his stomach to vomit out, yet he couldn't stop heaving, the puke spilling onto the cobblestones of the alley, mixing with his own blood.

"**You're a boy who has been plagued with darkness you don't deserve.**"

The sound of Lola's voice rang through his ears as he finally stopped, wiping some of the puke from the corner of his mouth.

Had he somehow manifested the darkness as a way to defend himself from Conli?

All he had done was think about his anger at the world, think about how unfair everything was, and how the gods didn't exist because what benevolent gods would allow so much suffering? He had thought about his own life, how he was alone and always would be. He took that anger, opened his eyes, and Conli had died.

No, not died. Killed by him.

He swallowed, a bloody, metallic taste, and tried to survey his injuries. He had at least one cracked rib, and his nose was most definitely broken, blood still gushing out of it. Those were the injuries he would need to address immediately. The rest were bumps and bruises, but they had impaired him.

He didn't want to move. But, as the boy glanced at the corpse, he knew he had to. If city authorities discovered that he was responsible....gods, he knew the boys would report him. He was in so much trouble now, he had just murdered someone. It was an act of self-defense, the boy thought, as he dragged himself to his feet using the wall. An act of self-defense in which the weapon used was seemingly his mind.

They would come for him because murderers were executed. That was the law, and he was now a murderer. His brain was foggy, his vision starting to fade, and there was a pounding in his head that wouldn't stop. He had to get out of here.

The boy managed to grab his pack, using the wall to guide him out of the alley.

As he was about to step out into the street, he caught a glimpse of Conli's body.

Seventeen years old. That's how old Conli had been. He was the creator of the misery throughout the boy's childhood, the leader of the gang who had driven him from the orphanage. Seventeen years old, no parents, who had been hardened by life so much that he felt the need to inflict pain on someone else. He hadn't asked to be an orphan either. Maybe he had a family who was trying to find him, a family trying to get back to him.

The boy should have felt terrible, awful, remorseful that he had just ended Conli's life in such a brutal way, in a way he didn't fully understand himself.

But he didn't.

He had the power to kill with his mind. And even though he didn't know how to control it, or even if it would happen twice, he knew this:

No one would ever hurt him again.

Chapter 1

Tilda, Orinth

"**D**id we make a mistake?"

They sat in a crowded tavern filled to the brim with loud, rambunctious sailors, smugglers, and townspeople who were shouting and laughing. She heard the question over the noise, echoing in her ears in a painful sort of way. She closed her eyes, wishing she hadn't heard the question at all.

Sahar gripped the mug in front of her tightly, her skin starting to go numb from the cold metal. She had ordered an ale but hadn't managed to take a single sip of it yet, only held onto it and let her hands freeze. She didn't respond to Roman, only stared at her mug and hoped he wouldn't repeat himself.

"Did we make a mistake, Sahar?"

She dragged her eyes upward finally meeting his gaze. Sitting across from Sahar, her old friend's drink was untouched, his fingers drumming the wood of the empty table they had managed to snag in their favorite tavern in Tilda. It was right on the sea, close enough that they could smell the salty air. The crew had been coming here since the very beginning of their operation and it had become one of many of their home bases, as Roman liked to call them. Normally, Sahar would sit at the bar, participate in drinking games, or get someone to sing on the stage so they could sing along. It was always a good time here.

But she couldn't bring herself to be normal. She couldn't participate in the fun that was around her. All she could do was hold onto her mug like it was anchoring her to the surface of the world.

Did we make a mistake?

Was it a mistake when we were paid to take an innocent, naïve girl named Nova Grey onto the ship, letting her come along on a trip to Nagaye?

Was it a mistake when every single one of them grew to like her immensely, when they began to enjoy spending time with her, watching her embrace their world aboard The Valley? Was it a mistake to welcome her with open arms to the crew, like a breath of fresh air they didn't know they needed?

Was it a mistake to not question her story, to accept that she had been telling the truth about who she was?

They had been at Louie's, one of their favorite bars in Aram. Sahar had been discussing business with one of her close allies, Eria Elliot, when Nova and Roman had walked in, both seemingly enjoying themselves. After briefly conversing with them, informing Nova she wouldn't have time to show her the town, Sahar had returned to Eria's side.

"Who is that traveling with you, Sahar?" Eria asked her.

Sahar slid back up onto her barstool, taking a long sip of wine before answering, "She's a passenger we picked up when we were in Rein. She paid us for passage to Nagaye, but she's more of a friend now." Even while telling Eria this, Sahar felt slightly disappointed. She had wanted to go shopping with Nova and take her to see the sights of Aram as she had promised. Normally, she enjoyed doing business but right now, it was the last thing she wanted to do.

"Nova?" Eria repeated, one eyebrow raised.

Sahar gave her a quizzical look. "Yes. Nova. Nova Grey. Do you know her?"

Eria gave a short laugh. "I do know her, not personally, and certainly not as Nova Grey. I think you will find most people recognize that girl as Princess Alida Goulding of Orinth."

Sahar blinked once, glancing at where Nova had just left the bar, before looking back at Eria. "What are you talking about?"

Eria tucked her blonde hair behind her ear and took another drink of her wine before replying, "I hate to tell you this, Sahar, but that girl sitting next to Roman was Alida Goulding, the princess of our country. I don't exactly know what's going on, but I've seen that face a million times and know it well. That's the princess."

"That's not possible," Sahar told her. "That's Nova. Her family is from Tenir. She's being sent to Nagaye by her parents to avoid the war. She told us about herself. She couldn't be lying about that. There's no reason to. Why would the princess pretend to be someone else to escape to Nagaye?"

"Maybe it's because there's a ransom the size of this establishment on her head."

Did we make a mistake betraying the girl we had come to know as Nova Grey, who was indeed the Princess of Orinth?

Did we make a mistake by handing her over to a group of Aunticans in exchange for bags and bags of gold, as much as they made in just a month?

Was it a mistake when they took her without giving any indication of what they were going to do with her and we let them?

Was it a mistake that we walked away after she had screamed they were going to kill her?

Was it a mistake believing that truly no harm would come to her, as the Aunticans promised?

Did we make a mistake?

She wanted to say no. She wanted to slam her fist onto the table and scream at her best friend that no, they hadn't made a mistake. They had done what they had always done, made a profit. They had talked about it so many times before they turned her over. Nothing was going to happen to her, they had said. She's a pawn in a political game. Nova put the crew at risk by boarding their boat. No, Alida. No, Nova. Who even was she? It didn't matter. They had no loyalty to her and the best thing for them to do was to turn her over, take the money, and forget about it. Of course, they hadn't made a mistake.

So why couldn't Sahar say that aloud?

Did we make a mistake?

"I don't know, Roman," she replied, and brought her drink to her lips, taking long gulps of it, hoping it would numb the intense guilt that was gnawing at her heart and mind.

"I just don't understand why she said that," he responded, fingers continuing to tap the wood, faster and faster. Sahar wanted him to stop. It was making her anxious because she knew that the small movement was the biggest indication that Roman was just as unsure as she was.

"Stop thinking about it," she told him. It was ridiculous and hypocritical, but she said it anyway.

"Why would she say that, Sahar?" Roman demanded, his voice growing higher. No one seemed to notice that the two of them were sitting there in complete misery. Most of her crew were glad to be off the sea, albeit briefly, and wanted to celebrate. They were drunk, or near that point. The last thing on their minds was the mental wellbeing of their captain and Sahar was glad for it.

"Roman, stop thinking about it."

"Explain it to me, Sahar. Why did she say that? I don't understand. I keep replaying it in my head and each time, it confuses me more and more."

Sahar slammed her mug onto the table with a loud bang. It rattled the other glasses and still, no one turned a head their way. Roman raised both eyebrows as she snapped at him, "Dammit, Roman. Do you really want to do this? We've gone over this a thousand times in the last two days. She's gone. Nova…Alida…whoever she was. She's gone. She's going to be fine. She's just a pawn in this, no harm will come to her. Why do we have to keep doing this?"

"Because you know as well as I do that she isn't fine," Roman said in a low voice.

Sahar stared at him. Through their years together, it was very rare he ever raised his voice at her. Ever. It was almost as rare that he spoke to her in an angry or upset tone. This was right on the edge of that. "How do you know that?"

"She told me the king is going to kill her, Sahar. She said he's going to spill her blood to open the Shadow Wall. It's one thing to make an excuse to get out of it. It's another to be that specific. Why would she say that about the Shadow Wall? Why?"

Sahar threw her hands into the air. "How am I supposed to know? She's a princess, Roman. She's proved to us how manipulative she can be. She blurted something out about being killed and blood and the Shadow Wall to try and trick us. Nova did it once. She probably thought she could do it again."

He was shaking his head, "You know as well as I do that isn't true. You didn't look into her eyes, Sahar. I did. I looked into her eyes, and I saw real and genuine fear for her life. Nova was afraid. She was truly afraid that she was being handed over. She knew it was more than a political game. She thinks she's going to die."

Sahar took a few deep breaths before responding. It would make no sense for them to get into an argument about this. She had to calm down and have a rational discussion. Roman was overthinking it. Alida was manipulative and she had managed to manipulate Roman into thinking she was in some sort of danger.

Not Sahar. No, Alida might've been able to fool her once, but not a second time. She was trying to trick them, even after she was out of their lives.

And as Alida's face flashed in her mind, her dark brown hair and brown eyes, her contagious smile and laugh that was as loud as it was endearing, Sahar realized this was about more than putting the crew in danger, or whatever excuse they made that justified turning her over to the Aunticans.

Sahar felt betrayed by Nova Grey.

She was the first female friend Sahar ever had. Making friends as a former prostitute turned smuggling ship captain wasn't exactly easy, and yet, she and Nova had spent countless, wonderful hours with one another on The Valley. Sahar loved talking with her, laughing with her, doing each other's hair and nails, getting drunk most nights, and cracking up over the stupidest things until tears ran down their faces. They had stood on the edge of the boat, the wind in their hair, and Sahar had told Nova about her husband and her past, something she rarely told anyone. But she had told Nova because Nova seemed like the type of person who would understand.

And she had. Nova had listened intently, not interrupting. When Sahar had finished, she hadn't tried to comfort her or apologize. She had called Sahar an inspiration to everyone, which was more touching than Sahar cared to admit. As much as their conversations were about silly things, Nova had opened up to her in return.

"Sometimes, I just feel trapped in my life," Nova once told her. "I feel like I'm not consciously making decisions. I think someone else is making them for me and I just have to deal with the consequences. I wish I could be someone else. Do you know what I mean?"

Sahar understood it now.

Your wish came true, Nova. You had gotten to be someone else.

But now, she was Alida Goulding once more, and Sahar had handed over this girl, who had been her friend, for profit.

What was happening in this world?

They had found out in the two days since being back in Tilda that there had been a battle on the border between Auntica and Orinth. Eria had mentioned that it was a battle that had held up her shipments for the black market, but more details had emerged. It had been a surprise attack by Orinth against Auntica. Orinth had won, massively, and the Auntican forces had surrendered. Now, the Orinthian forces were gathering in Lou, a border city to the North, anticipating another attack by Aunticans. The war was in full force and Sahar could hardly comprehend that.

On top of this, rumors had reached Tilda of an incident that had occurred outside of Tenir. In matters of the criminal underworld, word traveled fast. In this case, Jare Micheals, a close acquaintance of Sahar and prominent figure in the black market, had been involved, and therefore word had already reached her ear.

There had been eight bodies found outside the city without traces of a wound. No blood, no weapons, not anything. According to the rumors, a man from the Wilds had been kidnapped by a group of drunk Orinthians and was taken just outside the city. He had endured a beating, had been near death and the chances of his escape were completely impossible.

And yet, the bodies of eight Orinthian men had been found. The man from the Wilds had escaped and it was assumed he was responsible for their deaths. Jare had apparently been the one to stumble upon the scene and from that point on, the rumors had exploded.

Sahar didn't know how much of it was true and how much of it was rumors. A man from the Wilds being beaten up by Orinthians wasn't exactly a surprise. But being near death and managing to escape did not seem possible. There had to be someone else involved, Sahar had surmised when she heard the story. It was confusing, but Sahar also didn't think it was relevant to anything happening in her life.

Or maybe it was. When she heard the rumors, it struck something deep within her and she didn't understand it. Death happened constantly in the world of the black market. Why were these deaths any different?

Still, it nagged the back of her mind, along with the thousand other things that nagged her mind.

Like the fact that Nova Grey might die and it would be their fault.

Alida Goulding was going to die and it was their fault.

Sahar took a deep, shaking breath before finally responding to her first mate. "It was strange," she whispered, "the way the Aunticans ignored us when we asked who we had just given Nova—Alida to. I don't think it was the Auntican king, Grafph. I think we handed her over to someone else."

Roman bit his lip. "But who? The ransom was being offered by Grafph, we know that for a fact. Plus, the person who gave us the money was Auntican."

"But they were dressed in dark clothes. They weren't in an Auntican uniform, they weren't soldiers. Who were they and why were they the ones who were sent to get Alida?"

He shrugged, shaking his head. "Who did we give her to, Sahar?" In his voice was worry, pure and genuine worry, and Sahar wondered if there was something more behind Roman's desperation to find Alida. She had known him for a long time and had never seen him like this.

"We need to find out why Grafph wanted her in the first place," Sahar said. "I initially thought it was for a ransom. But Alida shouted out that he wanted to kill her, to spill her blood and open the Shadow Wall. You're right, Roman, that's way too specific to be some sort of manipulation tactic. But what in the world is she talking about? The Shadow Wall? Spilling her blood on it to open it? I don't understand."

"Nor do I."

"Did they already leave town?"

Roman nodded. "Some of the men reported a large group of cloaked soldiers being led by a woman. Alida was among them. They left soon after we turned Alida over."

Sahar scratched the back of her neck, feeling another wave of intense guilt. "Do we know where they were going?"

"North. And if I had to guess based on what Alida told us…" Roman inhaled deeply. "They're going to the Shadow Wall."

"To kill Alida," Sahar breathed, and that guilt was replaced by panic.

It didn't matter how betrayed she felt.

It didn't matter that she had been expertly manipulated by an eighteen-year-old princess.

It didn't matter that Sahar had been incredibly foolish by turning her over.

She would be guilty later. She would cry over it later. She would bang her head against a wall later.

Right now, there were more important things to do.

Sahar's head snapped up and she jumped to her feet. This time, it attracted the attention of some of the surrounding patrons. A few spoke to her, but she didn't hear them, just stared at Roman.

"Sahar?" he asked carefully.

"I know who we need to see," she said, and without another word, she ran out the door.

Chapter 2

Tilda, Orinth

2 days prior

The woman standing by the table had long, golden blonde hair that reached her navel. She was utterly beautiful, with the smoothest, pale white skin and blue eyes. Her lips were perfectly red, and she wore a dazzling gown, for some reason. Alida wondered if she was in a dream, as she observed the red, sparkly dress that Alida herself would've worn only for a ball. She wore a diamond necklace that Alida wagered was worth more than most people's homes. She stood straight, proud, and elegant.

"Who are you?" was all Alida managed to say as she took the woman in. It wasn't Grafph, nor his wife, that was for certain.

The woman frowned, still managing to stay gorgeous. "I'm surprised you don't recognize me, Alida, given that we share the same blood."

"What?"

The woman clapped her hands together, smiling. "Well, I suppose I shall introduce myself. My name is Cassia Messina."

"I don't know who that is," was Alida's first reaction to the beautiful woman in the second-floor apartment.

The woman, Cassia, rolled her eyes. "I'm sure that you do. Think about it." She walked over and sat across from Alida, crossing her legs and resting her chin on her hand, watching with amusement.

It was hard to think at the moment. Her head had started to pound due to the amount of escape attempts she had tried and the betrayal of Sahar and Roman only hours before. Oh, and the fact she was going to die for nothing. She had started this journey to get away from Orinth, yet here she was, still on the continent. She had gotten passage on a boat and thought she was on her way to Nagaye, only to find out her two friends had betrayed her and handed her over to Aunticans for a profit. She had figured out that she was not the Last Heir, but it was too late. She was captured and had exhausted all options of escape. Now, on top of everything, this Cassia Messina, a completely unrecognizable and slightly terrible person, was Alida's apparent captor.

And then it hit her. Cassia Messina. The human who had fallen in love with the demon. The cause of the Shadow Wall. The mother of the first half-blood, Arca.

But how? She had been alive hundreds of years ago. It couldn't be her currently sitting in front of Alida. There was no logical explanation.

"You're the one who fell in love with Abdiah." The room was starting to spin as Alida tried to get her mind wrapped around this reality. She held onto the table, staring at the woman.

Cassia's eyes flashed upon hearing the name. "Very good, Princess. That was me."

"How?" Alida managed to get out.

Cassia laughed and there was something so malicious about it that Alida shivered. "Such an easy question with such a difficult answer."

"You're the one trying to destroy the Shadow Wall?" Alida gaped.

She shrugged. "I suppose you could say that. Though the story around Orinth and Auntica right now is that Grafph is planning to demolish the wall."

Alida felt like she was going to throw up. Or faint. Or both.

"Grafph isn't responsible then."

"I never said that. It was quite easy to seduce him. Much too easy. He must already be an adulterer because it only took days. Once I had him telling me how much he loved me and needed me and all of that, I slowly planted my plan into his brain. Not using the shadow or anything of that sort, just good old-fashioned manipulation. And he did all of it, without even batting an eye. All of his advisors couldn't figure it out. Why did their king want the princess so badly? And then the diplomat from Orinth had to overhear us talking about the Shadow Wall." Cassia scowled at her, "This whole charade would have been over much sooner had you not run."

Alida glared. "How are you alive? You should be dead. You look like you could be a corpse come to life." She somehow knew the comment would get under her skin.

Sure enough, Cassia frowned at her. "That's not very nice, Miss Goulding. I'm not sure how old my soul is but in this body, I'm only thirty-eight."

"How?" Alida asked again.

Cassia shrugged again. "You won't believe it. You won't be able to wrap your tiny mortal mind around any of it, but I'll tell you because I'm finally ready to share the story of my success with someone and you're the lucky person. When I knew I was going to die, I made a deal with the gods."

Alida continued to listen without the slightest movement.

Cassia seemed amused by her apparent confusion. "Yes, Princess. The gods themselves. There are several ways to get in contact with them, and I did. I made a deal with them. I gave them something I loved, a sacrifice. It was difficult, but it proved successful. Instead of dying and going to the Beyond, I asked them to send me beyond the wall, into the Shadow Realm, where my love Abdiah had come from. Of course, the first thing I asked of the gods was to bring him back to me. They refused. It wasn't in their power, they said. But it was within the power of the Demon King."

Alida opened her mouth and closed it, unable to find the words to respond to all that she had just heard. She wasn't even sure she believed it.

"I found the Demon King, the ruler of the Shadow Realm since the wall went up. He took over and he rules all who dwell there, with the full power of the shadow. No one on this side of the wall knows the full extent of what lies beyond it. Aside from mortals like yourself, there are also shadow-beings. They are human in every sense of the word, but each of them possess the shadow. And then, of course, there are demons, but they are scarce. The most powerful is the Demon King. He has the power to summon souls back from the Beyond, into his realm. We made a deal. I would destroy the Shadow Wall, giving him access to this realm once more, and he would bring back my Abdiah. He will rule the world, I'll get my lover back, and we both get what we want."

Alida struggled to muster a response. Mentally, she was overwhelmed with the amount of information she was receiving all at once, on top of the panic Cassia had already given her. Shadow-beings? A Demon King? A deal with the gods? She couldn't keep any of it straight and she fought to keep from screaming in frustration. Instead, her mouth hung slightly open, in silence.

Cassia mocked her confusion. "You should be touched by that story. Don't all princesses adore passionate love stories? That's what it is darling."

Alida shook her head. "So, if I'm hearing this correctly, you're going to kill me and destroy the Shadow Wall because of a deal you made with a DEMON

KING, hoping he will somehow bring back your former lover from the Beyond, so you can grow old and die with him in a world plagued by demons."

Cassia frowned. "Well, I don't think I would put it like that. But yes, I suppose, if that's easier for you to understand."

"How do you know he isn't lying?"

Cassia chuckled, a low, gurgling sound that made Alida shudder once again. "I've spent the last thousand or so years in the Shadow Realm waiting for him to find a way to return me to the real world. And after a thousand years, he did. Do you know what being in the realm of shadows does to a human, Alida?"

Alida shook her head, suddenly very frightened of this woman in front of her.

Cassia smiled at her fear, standing up and walking closer to her. "I spent a thousand years in the Shadow Realm to get what I want. I would spend a thousand more without a thought. Trust me when I say the Demon King will not cross me. And neither will you, by the way. I know you're the Last Heir and you can summon the shadow too, but I've learned your powers will have no effect on me. And if you even try it, I'll show you the true meaning of pain."

Alida wasn't sure if now was the right time to insert the fact that she probably wasn't the Last Heir. Judging by the fire in Cassia's eyes, it was not.

"So, once I destroy the wall, I get my life back. You don't know what it's like to have it all in front of you and then have it torn into pieces. He made that sacrifice for me and our daughter. He made that sacrifice for this sorry excuse of a world. I'm just taking back what's ours."

Alida couldn't help herself. "You're crazy."

Cassia threw her head back and laughed. "Of course. The fool's response to anything is 'you're crazy'. You shouldn't talk to your family like that, Alida. After all, Arca is my daughter and your ancestor. You wouldn't be here without us."

"What was your side of the deal?" Alida asked, ignoring the painful reminder that somehow, regardless of whether she was the Last Heir or not, she was related to Cassia.

Cassia froze. "What do you mean?"

"I mean you said you made a deal with the gods. I don't know if I believe that, but deals are two sided. What did you give to the gods to send you to the Shadow Realm?"

Her eyes darkened once more and Alida sensed that there was pain there as she opened her mouth to respond, "I gave up something very dear to me, to the gods. That's all you need to know."

Alida wanted to push it. She wanted to know what it was that the woman had given up, because that meant she had a possible weakness. But the darkness in Cassia's eyes made her reconsider. "When did you come back to the real world?"

"I came back about five years ago, right when the tension between Orinth and Auntica began. Impeccable timing, really. What I was not anticipating was the Society of the True King getting in the way of my plans."

Alida remembered vaguely hearing the term from Ledger, the man she had met in the woods when her journey had only just begun. That conversation seemed like ages ago. She wished she were at his cabin now, eating venison stew and philosophizing. She wished she would've cherished those moments when she was free. "Aren't they harmless fanatics obsessed with the Shadow Wall and nothing more?"

Cassia snorted. "I wish they were only that. No, the Society of the True King has tried to track down any person they believe to be the True King, dating back to the creation of the wall. They weren't around when Arca was alive, but by the time her grandchildren were adults, they were seeking to kill the True King. They've continued doing that throughout the centuries."

Alida sighed in disbelief. "So not harmless."

Cassia shrugged. "I don't think they've ever succeeded. They've killed innocents before, because they've guessed the True King's identity incorrectly. But the Orinthian royal line continues and here you are."

She decided to just go for it. She was going to die either way, so might as well try. "So, you've heard of the True King," Alida said slowly.

Cassia's eyes flashed. "I have."

"And you still think my blood is going to open the Shadow Wall?"

Cassia smiled. "Yes, I do. Orinthian firstborns of the royal family. The Last Heir. But if I'm wrong, and I kill you for nothing, it doesn't matter to me. I've been waiting a thousand years to come into the real world. If it takes me a thousand more, I will find the Last Heir or the True King or whoever it is, and I will destroy the Shadow Wall."

"What if I told you I know for a fact it isn't me?"

"I wouldn't care." Cassia stood up, running a hand through her hair and arching her back to stretch. "I'm going to kill you either way, Alida Goulding, because you've been a thorn in my side. A few days after you left the capital city, I sent a team into the palace to kidnap you, but you were gone. I had to issue a continent-wide reward for your return to me, in Grafph's name. And then, I just had to pay that reward to two pirates or whoever they were. I don't care about money, but I care about time. You've cost me that, Alida, and for that, I'm going to kill you."

Alida laughed. "At least you have a good reason," she said sarcastically.

"Isn't it?"

"Where is your darling Grafph then?"

"He never left the capital. My men and I have done all the dirty work while my darling lover, Grafph, prepares for this battle. I couldn't care less about who wins this silly war, but I welcome the chaos. When the wall is destroyed, people are less likely to fight back."

"Aren't you Orinthian?" Alida asked in disbelief.

Cassia shrugged. "I suppose. There weren't really countries when I was alive. But Arca was the first queen of Orinth. I guess I am partial towards your country. But then again, I have been the lover of the king of Auntica for the last five years. I don't really care."

"You found a way to defy death. Your daughter, Arca, did she do the same? Is Arca alive?" Alida had been curious about the first queen of Orinth since hearing about the Last Heir. If there was a chance that the woman was alive, Alida had no doubt she would be fighting against her mother too.

The woman frowned and shifted uncomfortably. Alida sensed immediately that it was a sore spot. "No," she finally admitted, "she is not." That was all she said and Alida tucked the piece of information into the back of her mind. Cassia's sore spot was Arca, her daughter. There might come a time when she could use it.

"Were all of Arca's children demons then?"

Cassia shrugged. "There are some who believe any child born of a half-blood becomes a half-blood and has the power. Others believe it's only the firstborn. Regardless, you should be the Last Heir and that's a confirmed fact. The line began with the Orinthian royals whether there was a bastard child or not."

"Any chance you'll reconsider that it's me?"

Cassia threw her head back and laughed. Alida hated to admit it, but this woman, who was her ancestor, was beautiful, in a cold way, like the snow on a winter's morning. Pleasant to look at from a warm castle, terrible to get close to. "I'm beginning to like you, Alida. It's a shame I have to kill you."

"I mean, you don't have to," Alida argued. "I haven't used the shadow yet and I don't think I can. I truly believe that you're looking for someone else and not me."

"Didn't we go through this already?" Cassia looked down at a beautiful golden watch that adorned her wrist and whistled. "You had me talking, didn't you? We must go. I should change into something more suitable for travel."

"Where are we going?"

Cassia smiled. "Well, the Wilds of course. To the Shadow Wall." With that, she turned around, her red dress flowing behind her, and disappeared into the hallway from which she had first emerged.

Alida stood up immediately and tried the door again. Locked. She cursed under her breath and took a step back. With all of the weight and speed she could muster, she charged towards the door with her shoulder. She flew back onto the ground with a grunt. The door didn't budge and now her shoulder hurt. She checked the windows again. Barred. As if the bars would've magically disappeared from the first time she checked the windows. She didn't dare go in the direction that Cassia had just gone. There was no way out.

It was well and truly over then.

Alida sank to her knees, still wearing the clothes from the inn where she had hidden. That had been her mistake. She should have just left the city and figured something out on the way. She had been well-rested coming off the boat, besides the grueling swim to shore. Did she really need to stop to sleep and eat and get supplies? They had betrayed her twice. She told Roman the truth, that she was going to die, and he didn't care.

She pressed her face into her hands, trying desperately not to cry as the reality sank in once again.

Cassia Messina, the human that Abdiah had fallen in love with, the reason he had sacrificed himself to create the Shadow Wall, was going to destroy it. There was a weird sort of irony there. She was destroying the wall to get him back. She had made a deal with a Demon King. If Cassia was one thing, it was persistent. And also, an evil, despicable, manipulative person who Alida had no problem believing had spent a thousand years in a realm with other evil beings. And Grafph had fallen for it. He had been seduced by her and had decided to go along with her plan to destroy the wall. She made it seem like it was for the good of Auntica when really, it was for her own purposes. If Cassia had not come, it would have remained a petty dispute about gold. Now, there was an outright war between the two countries and the threat of a demonic invasion. Not the best set of circumstances.

She prayed to the gods that Rider was the True King, and that it wasn't her. She was afraid to die, but even more afraid that it would be her death to bring about the destruction of their world.

Rider didn't know it was Cassia who was seeking him out. Hopefully, no one knew he was the True King either. But the news about the Society of the True King worried Alida. No one had ever tried to harm Rider, so she didn't think they knew. But if the Society of the True King was aware of who he was, then it wouldn't take long for Cassia to figure it out.

The thought of Rider dying almost made her glad she was going first. She couldn't bear having to live after he was dead, especially considering it was his death that would destroy the wall.

Or at least she thought so. The weeks of sailing had given her apt time to think about it and she had come to the conclusion that it was him.

Why was she so confident about it? There was something about her faith in the answer that surprised her. She had no evidence that he was, besides the fact that he had the shadow, but anyone could. Why did she seem so sure?

She seemed to remember something that Ledger had told her, all those weeks ago in the forest.

"The way you talk about him, it seems like you could be family."

Her heart stopped.

No.

No, it couldn't be.

Rider had told her all about his childhood. Or at least a brief explanation of it. The reason he had gotten the job in the castle was because his father knew Tieran. But how did they know each other? Rider said that they had fought in the war together, but somehow it seemed impossible. By that time, Tieran had been the king. His advisor wouldn't have let the new king fight in the war, next to commoners. Her father and Rider's father wouldn't have met.

So how did they know each other?

If the line had managed to stay in her family for so long, her mother would have carried the burden of being the Last Heir.

Alida herself would've gotten it. Would've inherited the powers, the blood, the everything. But she didn't.

When she knew for a fact Rider did.

Rider had the shadow, and she didn't.

She knew of no one else who had the shadow.

Rider grew up in an orphanage in Tenir and had moved to Abdul when he was almost nineteen years old. He never explained the reason for moving. Only a few years after moving there, he had been employed at the castle, taken on as a scholar, a feat that was almost impossible, considering the lack of education or training he had.

Her father would not have fought alongside Rider's father. So why had her oldest friend gotten the job so quickly, with a complete lack of qualifications?

Because the queen was his mother.

No.

But it would make sense. Somehow, they had found each other, mother and son, and Natasha had brought him into employment to be close to him. If Rider really was her son, then he was a bastard child and could never be claimed as her kin. But if he were an employee in the castle, no one would suspect a thing. And Alida had to guess that no one ever did.

And then, her son saved his half-sister.

Alida.

She would've gotten the power. She would've gotten the shadow and been the Last Heir. It would've been her blood to destroy the wall.

But it wasn't.

Because her brother was born before she was.

"The way you talk about him, it seems like you could be family."

Rider knew and that's why he never stopped looking out for her. She thought they were good friends who bonded over their positions in the kingdom, but no. He was looking out for his little sister.

She wasn't going to see him again. Her brother. Her half-brother, but brother, nonetheless.

She was born eighteen years after him, when her mother was married to Tieran, and was considered the only child of the couple.

She had always described him like a brother. She loved him like one and all this time, it was true.

Why hadn't he told her?

Maybe he was protecting her. She felt ridiculously angry at him. He had promised there wouldn't be any more secrets, but at the same time she felt stupid. How hadn't she figured this out before, as soon as she had been informed about the Last Heir? She knew Rider had the shadow. She didn't know of anyone else who had it, not a single person. It should've been her first thought, instead of trying to figure how it could possibly be her. Lastly, she felt desperately sad. She knew now that Rider was her brother, and she would never see him again. It was a whirlwind of emotions and it was suffocating her.

Right as she was about to start either sobbing or screaming or both, Cassia returned. She had changed into better traveling clothes, a loose-fitting black tunic, her hair pinned up. For a woman who had been in a demon realm for a thousand years, she had aged well. She frowned at Alida.

"What's wrong with you? You look as if you've seen a ghost."

Alida swallowed back several retorts to that question. "Well, I'm going to die in a few days. I'm not exactly going to be cheerful, am I?"

"Look at it positively, Alida. You'll pass into the Beyond without ever having to worry about your world being fraught with shadow-beings. Isn't that a good thing?"

"Or I could stay alive and not have to worry about the world being fraught with shadow-beings. Ever think of that?" Alida didn't even understand what shadow-beings were exactly, but one thing she was sure of; she did not want them taking over her world.

Cassia laughed again and walked towards the door. She knocked on it a few times, in a specific pattern, and it opened. Alida cursed. Of course, there was some sort of secret code knock. Why hadn't she tried that?

Two guards, no longer Sahar's crew, entered. They were dressed in black cloaks and looked ominous. They both bowed to Cassia, from the waist.

"Boys, it's time to move out of this city and toward the Wilds," she ordered them.

They stood up. One of them opened the door for Cassia and she took his arm as they exited. The other dragged Alida off the ground, firmly but being careful not to hurt her. Without a sound, they followed Cassia and the man.

There were more men waiting in the alley, all on horseback, about twenty or so. There were three empty horses, and it was easy to guess which one was Cassia's. It was a beautiful white creature whose skin was almost glowing. She climbed up swiftly and patted its neck. The guard followed her onto another horse. The guard by Alida, however, grasped her waist and before she even had a moment to scream, hoisted her onto the horse. She landed with a small grunt and the guard climbed up behind her and grabbed the reins, putting her in a position where she could barely move.

Cassia glanced back at her and, satisfied, winked, before turning around and beginning to gallop toward the street.

Alida started bumping up and down as the horse she was on followed. She realized she was part of a giant group of riders surrounding her, with Cassia in the front, leading them. There was no possibility of escape, no possibility that someone would recognize her and call for help. It was over.

As they rode out of Tilda, a specific memory popped into her brain.

She had been fourteen years old. Her mother had been dead for several years and she was struggling to even remember the woman. It hurt her when she saw other girls and their mothers when she had a hard time recalling the face of hers or the sound of her voice or the warmth of her embrace. She had a particularly bad day and had hidden on one of the balconies, away from her father, Rider, or anyone else who would bother her that day. She had stayed hidden for hours before Rider tracked her down.

He didn't say anything, just sat down next to her. Without a word, she let her head fall onto his shoulder.

"What's got you down today, Lida?" he had asked her.

"It's not fair," she had said quietly.

"You're going to have to be more specific than that."

"No one knows what it feels like to be me right now."

"Oh yeah? And why is that?"

"All of these girls who are in our kingdom have their mothers. Mine is gone. It's just not fair. No one knows what it feels like."

Rider didn't say anything for a while, just let her wallow in sadness, before saying, "I know how you feel."

"How did your mother die, Rider?" she asked him.

He had given her a small, sad smile. "I don't know. No one ever told me. But I know how you feel. I'm sorry you're going through this, but I'm here for you. Always."

He had hinted at it many times, but he had never told her outright. In fact, the last night she was at the castle, he had told her his mother died when he was two. But no, Rider would have been twenty-six when her mother—their mother—died, from a disease that had ravaged her body.

He had told her no more lies then he had lied to her.

Why?

What was the benefit?

She wished that she could ask him. She would scream at him and yell and cry and sob and demand why he hadn't told her the truth. Then she would hug him and never let him go because she missed him and loved him so much. He was her best friend and had never done anything to hurt her. Everything he did was to protect her, and she had no doubt that keeping it from her was a part of that. She would always love him, no matter who he was or what he was capable of. She had watched him, twelve years ago, kill seven men with the shadow to save her.

"I'm not like the heroes in your stories, Alida."

She could feel in her pocket where his picture sat.

Where her brother's picture sat.

None of it made any sense.

She was going to die and none of these questions would have answers.

Alida looked down at her wrist and realized the bracelet that Ledger had given her was still there.

To remember the light.

She touched the bracelet and looked up to the sky, her head thumping against the chest of the guard behind her.

"I could use some light right now," she whispered, hoping someone, anyone, would hear her desperate plea.

Chapter 3

The River Iyria

He rode for three days straight before he finally had to stop. Without sleeping, eating, or resting, he had ridden, feeding energy to his horse using the shadow. He passed soldiers on the road, people fleeing from Lou, Aunticans fleeing Auntica, every sort of person imaginable, but he didn't stop for any of them.

Alida had been taken by Grafph and they were going to kill her.

They thought she was the Last Heir.

They were wrong.

How could he have been so stupid?

He should've never let her leave. He and Tieran both thought it would be protecting her, sending her to Nagaye, getting her off the continent and away from all the madness. Grafph was after her, and the farther away she was, the safer she would be. But they had been wrong. They should've anticipated how vast Grafph's reach was. Of course, he would catch her and now, she was in his hands. He was going to kill her and use her blood to open the wall.

It wouldn't work.

There was only one person whose blood would open the wall and it was him.

He knew he had the shadow since he was fourteen. He never knew how or why he had this power, but he used it and exploited it and made his life easier until he turned eighteen. He realized that it was a dark power that would ruin him. He made the decision to live honestly, without the shadow, even going as far to pretend he didn't have it.

It didn't work.

He had been nineteen years old, living in his own place in Abdul when his real father found him. After Rider had bought his own apartment in Tenir, he hadn't seen the man, but he didn't care. His father had left him to grow up in an orphanage, exposed to constant torment. Rider didn't want a relationship with him. Despite that, his father found him in Abdul. How he did this, Rider didn't know, but he decided to try to embrace the man. Maybe he could still have a family. What initially Rider assumed would be a social visit, turned into a truth visit.

"I'm here to tell you the truth, son," his dad had slurred, slightly drunk.

"About what?" Rider had asked.

"Who your mother is."

Rider paled when he heard the words. "You told me my mother died when I was two and that's why you sent me to the orphanage."

His father shook his head. "It isn't true. I'm sorry."

"Well, what's the truth then, Father? Have I had a mother this whole time who could've been raising me and instead I grew up in that nightmare in Tenir?"

"It wasn't my decision, Rider. There were people higher up than me, other things at play."

"You better explain before I lose it, Dad."

And he did.

His father had worked as a stable boy at the Orinthian castle from the time he was fifteen years old, hoping one day to be the head trainer. Princess Natasha Lyn, as she was known at the time, was passionate about riding. She was at the stables almost every day and they had become friends from the first time they met. When she was nineteen and he was twenty, it turned into something else: love. For the next two years, secretly, they were with each other. They spent as much time as possible with one another and there was no pressure to be anything other than themselves. When they were together, the titles disappeared. They weren't a princess and a stable hand; but a boy and a girl who just wanted a shot at happiness.

Until there was a baby.

It took her two months to realize she was pregnant with the child of the stable hand.

She didn't know who to confide in, so she turned to her grandmother, the former queen of Orinth who lived in Tenir. Pretending it was a sabbatical, without telling her parents the real reason, Natasha left Abdul and went to live with her grandmother for the next seven months.

Her grandmother was not a warm person. She was disappointed in Natasha and hesitant to help, but she knew what the stakes were. A scandal like this would ruin Natasha for the rest of her life, and the crown might be forfeited. So, she let her have the baby in secret. Her grandmother didn't just stop there, she sent the father to the War with the Wilds, hoping he would be killed. She took the baby, much to Natasha's dismay, to an orphanage in Tenir, to be raised by a stranger. The child would never know who he truly was.

It was all fine except her grandmother didn't know that Natasha possessed an evil and dark power called the shadow that had passed to her firstborn. As soon as the baby was born, a beautiful boy, he was ripped from Natasha's grasp before she even named him. The grandmother hid the boy and never told Natasha where he was. She left him at the orphanage and never looked back. All the while, the princess knew that somewhere, she had a child, and that child possessed the same evil she knew she had.

Natasha returned to the kingdom heartbroken and distraught, but couldn't tell anyone why. For twelve years afterwards, she was broken, unable to find her former lover or child.

The one thing the grandmother didn't count on was the father of the child living to tell the tale. The father confronted the grandmother and demanded to know what happened to his son. The grandmother refused to answer until he threatened to tell the entire world about the affair. The grandmother knew she could just have the man killed, but she was unaware what the consequences of his death would be. She told him the child's location. When the boy was about six, his father came to visit for the first time, but couldn't stay because he was a soldier. When the boy was nineteen, he decided it was finally time to tell him the truth because the War with the Wilds was intensifying and he didn't know how it was going to end. He had tracked the boy to his new residence in Abdul and told him everything.

Rider had been shocked into silence.

His father didn't know about Natasha's power, his mother's power. That's how he had come to have the shadow. He told his father this and he didn't believe him. Thankfully, by the next morning, he had forgotten, and Rider said goodbye to his father for the last time when he was nineteen. His father had been killed in the War of the Wilds.

It took him six years to work up the courage to face his real mother, who was the queen of Orinth. She had another child, another husband, another family. Rider was a part of the past, but when he finally worked up the courage, he went to the castle. He asked to see the queen and was denied, of course. He managed to bribe one of the servants to slip a note onto Natasha's breakfast tray that simply read: "I am your son". He had written where he could be found and the next day, unaccompanied by any guards, the queen had been at the door of his apartment.

They talked in private after this and he found out about everything.

Natasha told him about the shadow. It had awakened for her when she was twenty-one years old and the man she loved and the child she had were both taken away from her. She hadn't killed anyone, but the power had roared to life. She researched for months and found out the truth about the Last Heir and the True King and knew immediately. She was the Last Heir, and she was the True King. And now, her son was, and that was what terrified her. There was a boy who inherited the blood that could destroy the Shadow Wall and didn't know.

But now he did. And she had found him when he was twenty-five years old, but he was still her son.

They found a way to make it work. Tieran knew the truth now, too. Together, they formulated the story that Tieran and his father had fought in the Wilds together, despite the fact that Tieran had never seen actual combat during the War in the Wilds. His father died to save Tieran and that was why he let Rider come work for him. Rider would never inherit an actual position in the kingdom, or become a part of the throne. But he loved his job in the library, so it was never a problem for him.

Natasha had asked him one thing.

With tears in her eyes, she begged him, "I don't want Alida to know who you are."

At first, he was taken aback. It hadn't occurred to him that the young princess was technically his sister. His half-sister.

"I don't want her to know the extent of her mother's mistakes, that resulted in my awakening of the shadow. I don't want her to figure out that I almost ruined this kingdom for my family. If anyone would've ever found out about you, Rider, my family would've had to forfeit the crown. If Tieran would've known I had a son before he married me, he wouldn't have. I thank the gods he accepts me even now, knowing you're mine. I want you to be in Alida's life, just not as her brother."

He wished he could tell her, but he had agreed. It was his mother, after all.

He told Alida the lie whenever she asked him. And even after he promised he would never lie to her again, he told her the lie because it was his mother's wish and now, she was dead.

His mother's death was heartbreaking. It was so quick, and not one healer was able to save her. After she was gone, he felt an emptiness that he hadn't felt in years. Figuring out who his mother was, getting to be a part of a family, becoming advisor to the king, befriending Alida, all of it had made him whole again, after his teen years had almost destroyed him.

But Alida saved him after their mother's death. His little sister made him feel whole once more.

And now she was about to die, and she would never know the truth.

He was the one who was supposed to be killed. His blood, the blood of his mother before him and her father before her, would open the wall, not Alida's. He would let them kill him if it meant saving the person he cared about most in the world: his sister, Alida.

It was by the River Iyria, in Northern Orinth, where he finally collapsed off his horse.

His energy had run out. He had to sleep, and he had to eat. He would be no use to Alida if he couldn't move, couldn't fight, had no energy left to save her. He needed rest.

The guilt had eaten away at him, as well as the extent to which he had pushed himself. How could he have been so stupid? He felt his eyes droop close and his muscles relax at once as he drifted into a frightened slumber. Yet, underneath the surface of his skin, was the shadow, alive and awake. It was enjoying the sea of emotions he was going through. It was almost feeding off him, gaining more and more power. He tried not to pay attention to it. He tried to clear his thoughts, but it was impossible.

The truth was normally a social construct. The truth was made up by whoever was currently in charge. In Orinth, the truth was created by Tieran.

The truth that he had created for Alida was that she was an only child, the possible Last Heir. Before they had told her the truth, all those weeks ago, Tieran knew it was Rider himself who was the True King, and not Alida. But they had agreed that it was safer for her elsewhere. They also knew that if she believed there was a possibility she was the Last Heir, she would leave Orinth and not return until it was safe. If she knew the truth, she would've stayed and helped the fight and then Grafph would've caught her and it would've been over.

How wrong they were. How ridiculously stupid they were. They were dedicated to the memory of Natasha, the woman who begged them not to tell Alida the truth.

But Natasha was gone, and they should've just been truthful to begin with.

There was so much he hadn't told Alida, not just about their connection. There was so much he hadn't told Tieran. There was so much that weighed on his heart; he wondered if he could even bear it anymore. Part of him wanted to lay down and close his eyes forever and let the shadow consume him. Part of him wanted to take the knife strapped to his side and stab it through his chest until he bled out and then no one could ever open the wall. They would be safe.

It was only the thought of Alida that made him keep breathing and trying because he refused to let her die. Once he saved her, then he would figure out what to do, but she was the top priority.

He didn't know how long he slept but when he awoke, it was dark. His horse stood where he had left him, tied to a tree. He could barely see the creature, but the sound of the River was near. Iyria was the only river that ran through both Auntica and Orinth. He also knew that if he followed the river, it would eventually reach the Wilds.

He felt the picture in his pocket and pulled it out, using the shadow once again to track where she was.

He traced her mental scent immediately. It was impossible to tell exactly where she was from his powers. It never gave him a precise location or a clear picture, but from what he knew she was in the southern part of the Wilds. He let go of the picture and placed it back in his pocket, his power fading.

Rider felt around in his pack for some sort of sustenance. He cursed himself for not taking better care of his body. He would need all the strength imaginable to save Alida. He had no idea who was holding her, who would be guarding her, and who would be the one to kill her. Tieran had mentioned he didn't believe Grafph capable of sacrificing Alida, a girl he had known since her birth. So, Rider was wary of what he might have to face.

But if he had to give everything he was into the shadow to save her, he would. If he had to kill a hundred men to save her, he would.

He pulled out some jerky and forced it down his throat. It tasted terrible and made him feel sick, but he kept eating it because he needed the energy.

After choking it down, he laid back on the ground again and closed his eyes. His thoughts were racing, but he needed to sleep. He had been up for over seventy-two hours, fueled only by his rage and the shadow.

When he awoke, it was lighter outside, but giant storm clouds now lined the horizon.

Rider cursed and calculated how long he had until the storm would be upon him. Already, the winds were furiously blowing the trees around him, his horse neighing loudly for help. Rider rushed towards him and untied the rope around the tree. He tried to stroke his nose to calm him. It didn't work. The storm clouds were intimidating and making him antsy.

"Calm down, Starlight," Rider said, recalling the name Alida had given the horse with a pang of sadness.

The horse did not calm down, but Rider had no choice but to mount him in this state. The storm clouds stretched across the sky, darker than any storm he had ever seen. It was like the world was anticipating the evil that was about to transpire. He wanted nothing more than to take cover from the storm's fury, but he couldn't. Rider kicked Starlight in the side, and they took off galloping, following the banks of the River Iyria.

He remembered the day he saved Alida almost as if it was yesterday.

Natasha had burst into the library, shrieking for him, tears streaming down her face as Tieran followed. Luckily enough, there was no one else in there to witness the scene.

"Rider, they took her," Tieran said quietly. "They took her."

The queen was wailing unintelligibly so Rider asked, "Took who?"

"Alida. A group of rogues from the Wild took my daughter."

Rider took a couple deep breaths to calm himself. His sister. He still wasn't used to the notion. Alida had darted in and out of the library a few times to get different books and he had always helped her eagerly. But he had heeded the queen's word. He wouldn't tell her their connection and he wouldn't force her to have a brotherly-sisterly relationship with him. If it happened, it happened, but he wouldn't be the cause of it.

He turned to his mother, who was also calming herself with deep breaths. "Why didn't you use your powers?" he whispered, quiet enough that even if there were passersby, they wouldn't have heard.

She sobbed, "I've never used it before, Rider. I know it's there, but I've never let go of the restraint and let the shadow do its will. I was afraid I might hurt Alida if I unleashed it. I've never killed before with it and I didn't want to take the risk."

He nodded, feeling slightly nauseous at the prospect of using the shadow. It had been a long time since he had used it, but they had taken his mother's daughter. His sister.

He left the castle from the servant's entrance, where no one saw him leave. He found the wrecked carriage right where Natasha said it would be. He picked up an arrow and used it to find where the men were hiding out. Rider had once stayed in those very same caves before moving into Abdul and knew exactly where to go.

He tracked them down and killed the first man in front of the cave without even thinking about it.

It had been a long time since he had killed, but the skill returned to him immediately. The shadow was happy to devour these men who had taken the princess.

He killed another two before he picked up Alida. She had looked at him with such fear in her eyes that it almost ended him right there and then. He wanted her to like him, desperately. The only way they were ever going to have a relationship is if she chose to start it. He wasn't supposed to tell her, and he wouldn't, but she could still befriend him. It was still possible.

Rider killed the rest of the men and explained to the princess that she couldn't speak a word of what had happened to anyone.

He returned the princess to her parents.

When she leapt from his arms into theirs, he went to leave before stopping and turning around, his breathing heavy.

"Never," he said slowly, emphasizing the word. "Never force me to use my power again."

His mother, the queen, with Alida squirming in her arms, stared at him, tears in her eyes. Tieran watched him as well, with a little more hesitation.

"We won't," the queen promised him.

It was then when the king made him an advisor. They had never once even mentioned his powers after that. It would've been so easy to ask him. The shadow had many uses that would prove indispensable to a king: using mind games on opponents, wiping out enemies, becoming an assassin. But after Rider's request, they stopped talking about it completely. They pretended Rider was a normal person and for that he was glad. Yet, he saw it in their eyes, sometimes, when they thought he wasn't looking. He saw their fear, their disgust at what he was capable of. Rider couldn't understand why; Natasha was capable of the same. But it was one thing to have it; it was another thing to see it in action. He had murdered those seven men in the caves and worse than that, they hadn't been the first he had killed.

Alida was the only one who looked at him the same. Then again, she had only been six and not old enough to understand the implications.

She was now.

After he had saved her, the little girl became attached to him. She became like an actual little sister, one whom he adored. He often wondered if somehow she had figured it out, had discovered their connection as brother and sister, and was trying to have that relationship with him. But she never did.

Rider would tell her. He would tell her as soon as he saw her next, because he was going to see her again. He was going to save her and then reveal that they were brother and sister. He would not let her die. He refused to let her die. For that reason, he continued riding.

The storm was growing worse. The harsh wind had turned into waves of rain, pounding against his face and his horse. It was growing harder and harder to see as it limited his sight to whatever was directly in front of him. He could hear the rushing waters of Iyria, but now it was louder, the rain pounding against it. His horse was struggling to move against the wind and the rain, and he prayed to the gods to make this stop. It was slowing them down and they weren't even in the Wilds yet.

A crack of thunder shook the ground which made Starlight buck in fright. Rider wasn't prepared for it and the horse threw him off his back. Rider landed in a heap on the wet ground, rain continuing to pound down as he heard Starlight take off running. He cursed and tried to get up, but it was almost impossible with the strength of the wind. When he saw a bolt of lightning, he knew it was time to take cover. There would be no riding in this; that would mean death. He would have to find Starlight and find some place to get out of this weather. He knew they were nowhere near a village. He would have to find some sort of cave or something to protect him, at least from the lightning. Struggling to remain upright, he took off after Starlight.

The horse hadn't made it very far and was cowering under a large tree close to the river. Rider grabbed him by the reins and immediately calmed him with the shadow, enough that he could control him. Pulling him, they started running. Rider looked for anything to protect them. It was times such as these he wished the shadow worked against the natural elements. Give him an army of men and fine, he could take them all out. But he was utterly defenseless against this storm, as any other person would be.

In the blur of the storm, he saw it. The river had transformed into a small pond and, on the other side of the shallow pond, was a cave. He couldn't tell how large the cave was from here but, at the very least, he and Starlight could take turns taking cover. This was his only chance.

Leading a braying Starlight, Rider ran towards the cave, the water stinging his face. Another crack of thunder shook the ground and lightning cracked, coming so close it lifted the hair on his neck.

"Come on, Starlight!" he yelled.

As he got closer, he realized there were two figures standing at the mouth of the cave, watching him and shouting. He couldn't hear what they were saying because the wind was roaring in his ears, but he hoped they were encouraging him to join them in the safety of the cave. He didn't have time to be surprised that there were two other people near the border of the Wilds. He pushed forward. One of the figures was small and the other was much larger. He gasped for breath as he ran, Starlight forcefully trying to tear himself free. Rider once again used a wave of the shadow to make him come.

He could hear them more clearly now. Auntican.

"Come on! Get out of the storm, come on!" The accent was thick, and it worried him. What good could he run into by sharing a cave with someone with a thick Auntican accent? But strangely enough, it sounded like a woman's voice.

He was ten feet away when he could see their faces.

One of them was a large man, with a serious face, but with worry in his eyes. He was taller than Rider by a few inches with a broad chest and shoulders, an indication of his strength. He had brown hair soaked with rain and wore strange clothes that Rider had not seen before. The man was kneeling, waving at Rider to join them in the cave, shouting things in a language that he hadn't ever heard before. Rider pressed forward.

The other face...

She was a head shorter than the man and had blonde hair that just touched her shoulders.

But the face.

It was the face Rider had seen every time he closed his eyes at night. It was the face that haunted him throughout his days, following him in his dreams, screaming in his nightmares. It was the face that long ago had held his heart, made him feel as if everything in the world was going to be alright. The face that he had fallen in love with when he was a boy in Tenir. It was the face that made him realize he had a life outside the shadow. It was the face he ran away from because he couldn't bear to live with himself if something happened to her. It was the face that he never let himself go back to, no matter how much he wanted to, needed to. It was his biggest weakness, the one with the capability to destroy him. He had loved her so much that he ran away because when you love something, you want to keep it safe, and loving him never made you safe.

He fell to his knees, letting go of Starlight's reins.

The breath was knocked out of him, his eyes widened as he screamed. "MARVIE!"

Chapter 4

A Village in Orinth

Two days after she had murdered eight men, Sawny and Adriel finally stopped to rest.

She had gotten a room for them in the next village they came across, small enough that they would take any business they could get, regardless of the customer. The innkeeper didn't bat an eye at her companion from the Wilds, just sold them the room without comment. Sawny had thanked him profusely, much to his confusion. To him, it was just business, but to Sawny, finally some peace. They could get a good night's rest for once, in a bed, both of them.

Wait.

Sawny turned to Adriel as the innkeeper walked into the back to get their key.

"I only got us one room," she whispered. The small inn also acted as the village's only tavern and was currently packed to the brim with people. Sawny smelled something delicious and with one look at the house ale, she knew she had to have a glass later.

Adriel raised an eyebrow. "Oh?"

She elbowed him playfully. "I can get another one for you if you want."

"Is that what you want, Sawny?"

She blushed furiously. "Stop."

He gave her a wicked smile. "I'm only joking. I'll take the floor of whatever room we get."

She shook her head. "Yeah, no. I don't think so. It's your turn to have the bed on this journey."

"Let me be a gentleman and take the floor."

"Are you sure?" she asked him.

He smiled back at her, his gorgeous smile that never failed to make her heart beat a little faster. "I'm sure."

Before she could speak again, the innkeeper came back with a key. "Come down for dinner whenever you like. We stop serving at two in the morning. It's free with the room," he spoke Orinthian and glanced at Adriel again, "and your husband is welcome here too. No one will bother him."

Sawny opened her mouth to protest, then closed it. "Thank you," was all she said, taking the key from him.

Adriel picked up their bag and they started towards their room on the first floor down the hall. Sawny unlocked it with the key. It was large and spacious, with a gigantic bed in the middle. The other half of the room had a small dining table with two chairs, a large bathtub and basin, and a wide window, giving them a view of the village outside.

Adriel whistled. "In my life, I've never stayed in a place as nice as this."

Sawny sat down on the bed. "I didn't know Orinthians were capable of something this nice."

Adriel laughed. "I thought you were done with Auntica."

She scoffed, "After what they did to you, I'm not exactly hot on Orinth right now."

He sat down next to her, shoulders touching. "Me neither."

She had been adamant on him stopping and resting every chance they got. She personally had changed his bandages and made sure he ate as much as he could. It had been a day and a half since they left the outskirts of Tenir and Adriel was already starting to look better. The cuts on his arms had disappeared and his eye was no longer swollen. The wound on his abdomen would no doubt leave a scar, but the important thing was that he was alive and breathing.

Sawny hadn't processed what had happened yet. One minute, she had been in the library, discovering the truth about who her mother was, as well as the name of her birthfather. The next, she had been riding furiously to save Adriel, who had been kidnapped by a group of drunk Orinthians. They had beat him to the point of death, and tied him to a tree, no doubt intending to kill him. Sawny had tracked them outside of the city and attempted to smuggle him away, only to be caught by the leader of the group, and almost killed herself.

Yet she had been saved.

Not by weapons. Not by Adriel. Not by Jare, the man that had seen Adriel's capture.

But by an evil power that she possessed deep within her, that had been awakened and summoned by a feeling of anger so intense, it had exploded. That explosion resulted in the bodies of eight men. The sensation of killing them was indescribable, like waking up after years and years of being in deep slumber. She recalled learning about the shadow only hours before, a dark, evil power that came from beyond the wall, and she had no doubt that she possessed it herself.

How she possessed it? Why she possessed it? What she was supposed to do now that she had awakened this power? Those were all questions she couldn't answer and it was terrifying. She was lost and confused.

But she had Adriel. He had looked into her eyes after she confessed the manner of her killing, and he had promised he wasn't going to leave. He saw the darkness within her and was by her side nonetheless. Sawny didn't know what she was going to do. But for now, her goal remained the same. She was going to help Adriel find his brother's killer. And then, harness the power she had awakened to kill the man herself.

Because right now, the man sitting next to her, this warrior from the Wilds who she had come to know, had come to care about immensely, was the most important person in her life. She would solve his case, kill his brother's killer, and then go from there.

"How have you been feeling?" she asked him.

"You ask me this almost every hour, Sawny Lois," he said jokingly.

"It's because I care about you!" she protested.

Instead of responding, he replied, "I'm getting hungry. Do you care enough about me to go get some food?"

"Don't ignore the question."

He sighed dramatically. "I'm fine. I swear. I feel much better. The wound only hurts sometimes. My eye sometimes doesn't see, but that's rare. I promise you I'm fine."

She placed her hand onto his leg and said, "Good, I'm glad."

"And what about you?"

"What about me?"

He covered her hand with his own. "How are you feeling?"

It had been a whirlwind of emotions the past two days. Sometimes she woke up screaming because she could see each and every one of their faces, the men she had destroyed. Other times, she could feel the power boiling beneath her, wanting desperately to strike, but she tried to block it out. It gave her a splitting headache and made her muscles burn, but she had managed to stop it. The worst part was the not knowing. She had no idea how she had come to have this power, or what it was. She suspected it was the power behind the wall, but what did it mean? There were so many questions floating around in her head that she had no idea how to find answers to.

On top of that, the newfound revelation of who she was, who her mother really was, and the secrets of her past weighed down upon her like a heavy burden. It caused her even worse headaches than her power did. All in all, it felt like her brain was being torn in two, between the mystery of who she was and why she was capable of evil things.

"I'm fine too," she managed to say.

Adriel rolled his eyes. "You're a terrible liar."

"No, really!" she insisted. "I am!"

He turned to her, tucking a loose strand of her hair behind her ear. "It's okay to not be okay, Sawny. I know how confusing it is, but we're getting closer to my answers. As soon as we get them, then we'll work on your answers."

She smiled at him, "Okay. Okay."

They ended up camping that first night after the nightmare in Tenir. Sawny was terrified, but Adriel had insisted it would be alright. After building a small fire, they had camped near a large river called the Dela. Sawny had sat down and told him everything.

She let him read all of her notes and then the letter her mother had sent her. She explained as best as she could without breaking down what happened after she went to look for him. She told him in detail what had happened with the men who had been holding him hostage. He had been sitting across from her, the fire dancing in his eyes. He hadn't said a word the entire time, just watched her. When she finally finished, he said nothing, but embraced her and held her for a long time.

She hadn't been crying. She refused to cry again, but it was nice to be in his arms.

"I owe you my life," he had whispered in her ear.

"You owe me nothing."

He pulled back and stared into her eyes. "No. I owe you my life, Sawny."

She looked down at the ground and then back up at him. "I would do it again in a heartbeat."

Then, she explained to him who she believed had killed his brother.

Of the many theories that was in the book she read, the one that seemed the most likely to her was about the king's mysterious advisor. She didn't know his name, but it wouldn't be hard to find out. It was a young man in his twenties who started out in the castle working in the library. A year later, without any explanation, he was promoted to the king's head advisor, almost immediately after the princess of Orinth was saved from the caves. Now, there was no proof of this, but there had been sightings of a man walking by himself towards the caves. There was gossip among the servants of the royal household that he had walked in carrying Alida.

There would be no other reason a man, a low-level servant, would be promoted to the advisor without some explanation.

She wasn't sure enough to let Adriel kill him, once they found him.

But she wasn't scared of his power anymore, if the advisor had it. Because she had the same power that was wild and untamed and would protect Adriel at all costs.

She believed it was this man who was the True King.

Tomorrow morning, they would ride to Abdul, to the castle, and track down the man. She didn't know how she would be able to meet him and planned to figure it out as she went. She wasn't sure how effective this could be. Even if she did manage to find him, he would probably never confess to killing the men in the caves, but Sawny was hoping to catch him by surprise. She had become adept at reading people and if he gave any indication he was lying, she would figure it out. And if she needed to, she would use the shadow to get her answers. Not that it would help. If he really was the one she was looking for, he could match her powers. If he did confess, she would leave and tell Adriel. Whatever happened after was up to him.

If Adriel decided he wanted to kill the man, Sawny would help him with no questions asked.

Adriel disapproved of the plan and she knew it, but he didn't say so. She could tell by the look in his eyes and the set of his shoulders. He didn't protest or even beg to come with her because he knew she could protect herself much better than he would ever be able to.

After whatever happened in Abdul, Sawny didn't know what would come next.

Of course, there was her business back in Illias. She found herself missing her apartment, missing her giant desk and her cases. After she finished in Abdul, she could finally go back and start finishing the rest of her open cases.

Adriel was planning on paying her, despite the change in their relationship, and that money would drastically change the way she operated.

She knew where she would be after they were done. She would go back to Illias.

What worried her was what would happen to Adriel afterwards.

If he succeeded in killing the True King, the man who killed his brother, he could return to the Wilds. He wouldn't have to live in fear of exile anymore. He could go home, after five years, and finally bring closure to his people.

The thought of it filled her with such joy and such sorrow.

She had become pleasantly used to him in her life. To watch him leave it, after all they had been through together, would hurt. He promised he wouldn't leave her, but how could she keep him from going back to the place he loved, his home?

She wouldn't.

Sawny wasn't aware that she had zoned out in her thoughts until Adriel nudged her.

"Everything alright?" Adriel asked her.

She tried for a reassuring smile and failed. "Perfect."

"Sawny?"

She sighed and laid back on the bed, staring up at the ceiling. "I just...I don't know what's going to happen when this is all over."

"What do you mean?"

"I mean what's going to happen to...to us?"

"Us?"

"I'm going back to Illias after this. What little life I have is there: my business and my home. And you'll be going back to the Wilds, whatever happens. I'm just afraid after that there will be no us. I mean, when this started you were just my client, but after everything that's happened? You've seen me kill, what, ten people? Maybe more. A forest witch took over my brain. You were attacked by Orinthians and almost beaten to death. This isn't the normal experience my clients have so don't judge me too harshly. I just don't think I can go back to normal after all of that."

Adriel was quiet for almost a minute before his shoulders started shaking. Sawny realized he was laughing.

She smacked him lightly on the shoulder. "Adriel! I'm serious!"

"I know you are, Sawny, but that is the most ridiculous thing I've ever heard."

She opened her mouth to respond but he held his hand up. "Let me explain. I told you when we were outside of Tenir that I'm not leaving you. Even after everything that's happened. Sawny, I don't even know that when we find this man, the king's advisor or whoever it may be, that I will kill him. I don't know if I want to go back to the Wilds. I have no one up there anymore, besides my sister. I don't want to settle there. It's not home to me. Like I said before, for some reason or another, we found each other. By luck or by chance, but we're here together now, and unless you use your shadow power to blast me off this land, I'm not leaving you."

"I might stay in Illias. I don't think I'll relocate my business."

"I would go with you to the ends of the world if you asked me."

She smiled at him as he leaned back next to her.

"What if I told you I've always wanted to live in Tenir, Orinth?" Sawny asked him.

Adriel shuddered. "Even there, Miss Lois, even there."

She tucked herself into his side. "Thank you for saying all of that, Adriel. It means the world to me. I wish I could explain it."

He rested his head on hers and was silent for minutes afterwards.

"Let's go get something to eat," he finally said, sitting up. He extended a hand down to her and helped her up. Together, their hands woven, they went downstairs.

The dinner was extremely enjoyable and made Sawny feel like she was just a regular, normal person with a regular, normal life. She was at dinner with this perfect man, smiling, laughing, talking. The food was delicious and there was no trouble, not even a strange look at Adriel. Instead, they just enjoyed each other's company. It wasn't the first time on this journey that she wished she could pause the moment and make it last forever.

That thought abruptly left her mind when a man burst into the inn frantically and yelled.

"THE PRINCESS!! SHE'S BEEN TAKEN!"

Sawny had been in the middle of taking a sip of soup when he yelled it. The entire inn, which was crowded with people, fell silent and stopped to look at the man.

The innkeeper looked livid. "What in the name of the gods are you talking about?" he demanded furiously.

The man, who was actually more like a young teenager, was clearly out of breath. Sawny realized it was the innkeeper's son, who had helped them with their horses. "The princess, Alida Goulding. She's been taken by Grafph."

Sawny felt her heart stop.

"Who said so?!" a patron demanded.

He turned to him. "The news has spread like wildfire. It was a Vacci who turned her in and now they're going to kill her in the Wilds as an act of revenge against our king."

Sawny dropped her spoon and it clanked when it hit the table, loudly. No one looked at her. Their entire attention rested on the boy.

No one spoke until the innkeeper did. "It's going to be okay. Tieran will send someone to save her. She will be fine."

The boy shook his head. "I don't think so, Father. I don't think so."

The noise in the tavern resumed, but it was hushed, every patron suddenly discussing the princess. The entire air of the place had changed, from enjoyment to worry.

Adriel spoke softly, "I don't like the Orinthian princess, but they care about her so much. It's almost touching."

Sawny turned to him as the buzz across the room grew louder. "Adriel, we have to go save her."

Adriel looked dumbfounded. "What?"

"We have to go save her," she repeated.

She didn't know why but there was a feeling in her gut that told her she had to save the Orinthian princess. Grafph was going to kill her because he thought she was the Last Heir when really, she had no powers, no demon blood, and would be killed for no reason. She was innocent. But why did she care if the princess of her enemy country was killed? It was unfortunate, but it wouldn't have any effect on her life. The wall wouldn't open if her blood was spilled. In the grand scheme of things, her death was nothing.

So why did Sawny feel utterly panicked about the notion of her being murdered?

"Why? Why do you want to save her?" Adriel asked. He didn't sound upset or angry but confused.

Sawny shook her head, "I don't know. I don't know. I know she's not the True King, but we have to. We have to go save her. Something is telling me we have to."

Adriel leaned back in his chair. "Always listen to your instincts. I was taught that as a young child."

"Well, my instincts are telling me we need to leave now."

"We already paid for the room. We could stay the night and leave tomorrow."

Sawny shook her head. "We need to leave now, or we'll be too late."

Adriel stood up. "I just got done telling you I would follow you anywhere, Sawny. I'm a man of my word so let's get our stuff and go save the Orinthian princess."

Sawny stood up and grabbed his hand. "Are you absolutely sure you're okay with it? It will take time away from your case and we'll have to go to the Wilds. That's where they're going to kill her, at the wall."

Adriel squeezed it. "Yes, I'm sure. I'm not letting you go alone either. I know the Wilds like the back of my hand, and I also happen to know where they will try to kill her."

"What? Where?"

"There's a part of the wall where there is this flat stone that's raised up. It looks almost like an altar. No one has ever known what it was for, but once you told me about the Last Heir and the sacrifice, I knew. They were using it for that. I know right where it is."

"Then let's get going."

They ran upstairs, leaving half-eaten meals behind and Sawny laughed bitterly inside. They couldn't even make it through a dinner without something happening. Of course, she didn't have to go save the Orinthian princess. She had no idea how she would even pull it off, but something told her if the princess died, there would be unspeakable consequences. She wasn't frightened though. She could kill people with her mind. What did she have to be afraid of?

Within an hour, they were back on their horses, bags repacked, in new traveling clothes, everything replenished. They hadn't gotten the chance to sleep, but she knew they couldn't stop. They were far from where they needed to be. They had to ride for days straight until it was absolutely necessary to stop. She told Adriel this, who responded with a nod. He had turned back into the warrior from the Wilds, instead of the relaxed man, but she was glad. She didn't know what to expect when they reached their destination. An alert warrior was just what she needed on her side.

They rode for two days, across the Dela and north of Abdul before they had to stop. The horses were exhausted, and they were as well. She managed to force Adriel to change his bandages before they both collapsed onto the ground in sleep, without a fire or a blanket. Hours later, they awoke and began riding again, as replenished as they could be.

It was the most ground she ever had to cover on horseback, in the shortest amount of time. They rode faster than she ever had before. Every moment that passed, she feared the princess was already dead, but she couldn't understand why she feared it. She was Auntican for gods' sake, but the idea of the girl being dead filled her with a dread she couldn't comprehend.

They stopped after another day in Northern Orinth, near the border with Auntica.

This time, they had made a proper camp, with a fire and actual food. Adriel had reminded her that they would be no use to the princess if they were drained of all their energy and she agreed. A longer period of rest would give them the boost to finish the journey as well as fight if they needed to. The air of the journey had changed. There was a sudden urgency that filled her as well as Adriel. He felt her fear, her dread, and her panic and realized what was at stake. He didn't care if it was the princess of the country that hated him; he did it for Sawny and if she would've had any room left in her brain, she would've marveled at how absolutely incredible he was.

When they awoke the next morning, there were storm clouds on the horizon. They were just south of the border of the Wilds, according to Adriel, who had been leading them.

Adriel looked warily at them. "That's not good."

Sawny followed his eyes. "It looks like a storm."

He chuckled, no joy in the sound. "Trust me, storms up here are nothing like storms in Auntica. We're almost to the Wilds and this is a Wild storm."

"What do we do?"

"We need to take cover immediately. I know you want to keep moving but if we get stuck in the storm, it could mean death."

"I believe you. Let's go."

They rode as fast as they could, looking for some way of staying out of the storm, as the clouds came upon them. It started as a light sprinkle before the skies opened up and began to drown the world in rain. Luckily, Adriel spotted a cave from a distance, and in the wind, they rode towards it. It was incredibly difficult, and the horses were starting to panic, but they pushed on. The cave was across a pond. Together, they jumped off the horses and ran towards the mouth of it, dragging the fighting beasts behind them.

The cave was huge and empty, almost as if it had been previously occupied. Adriel confirmed that notion.

"This was a gathering place for the tribes of the Wilds," Adriel explained. "The caves were sacred spaces for us. All the elders and the tribal councils would gather here so it had to be large. They would empty everything out. They had to abandon it after the war."

Sawny tied Indira to a rock as far away from the mouth of the cave as she could get, to lower her chances of running away in fear. She stroked her horse's nose, whispering in her ear to soothe her. It worked, but barely. Adriel had tied his horse nearby, but walked back to the mouth of the cave, eyeing the situation outside. The rain still could be heard from the top of the cave and all of them were soaked to the bone. Sawny shivered. She patted Indira one last time before returning to the front of the cave, where Adriel was now sitting.

She sat down next to him. "This sucks," she said plainly.

He agreed. "This is not great."

"I'm sorry," Sawny sighed.

He looked at her. "For what?"

"I can't think of a single reason I'm loyal to the princess of Orinth, Adriel. We've just spent multiple days riding up here to save her and for all we know, she could be dead. I just don't understand why I feel like this."

"I trust you, Sawny. Trust yourself. I'm sure whatever the reason is, it's good. Plus, the princess is only eighteen. She doesn't deserve to die. She isn't the True King, and her blood won't open the wall. Why does she have to die?"

"You're right, she doesn't deserve to. But still, I've killed so many times before. It shouldn't bother me that one more person is about to die."

Adriel stood up. "I wish you could see yourself the way I see you."

Sawny stood up next to him. "I don't understand."

He turned to her, fully facing her. "You're a good person, Sawny. I see it every time I look at you and I wish you did too."

She shook her head. "But I'm not. I've never been. It's just who I am."

He rolled his eyes. "Sometimes talking to you is like talking to a brick wall."

She laughed, despite the situation they were in. "I'll take it as a compliment."

"Do you trust me?" he asked her.

"Of course, I do."

"Would you trust me with your life?"

"Yes. Instantly."

"Then trust me when I tell you that you're a good person."

A giant crack of thunder shook the cave as she stared up into his blue eyes. "I am when I'm with you. You make me want to be a good person." He blinked once and a small smile crept onto his face as he wrapped an arm around and pulled her closer. They were chest to chest, face to face, and she could feel his breath against her skin as she closed her eyes. Her heart was beating so hard in her chest and her hands were trembling. Sawny opened her eyes, bringing her forehead to touch his own.

And then, she kissed him.

It was the most wonderful thing she had ever experienced. His lips pressed against hers, searching, needing, feeling, exploring. She let her hands tangle up in his shirt, pulling him close enough so there was no space between them. He ran a hand through her hair and tilted her head back. She let out a soft breath as they continued, and she was in paradise.

It was minutes before she pulled back, breathing deeply.

Adriel stared at her, his expression one of shock and joy. "Wow."

"Good or bad wow?" she asked him.

He smiled so big at her that she was tempted to grab him by the shirt, pull him to the back of the cave, and forget about the war and the journey and all of it.

"Good wow," he breathed, his shoulders moving up and down, and she wanted nothing more than to press her lips against his again, for as long as this storm would last.

Sawny exhaled, laughing. "Well, let me tell you this…"

She didn't get to finish as she heard a horse let out a loud bray. It wasn't Indira or Adriel's horse, though. It had come from outside of the cave. Both of their heads snapped towards where the sound had originated.

Adriel knelt to the ground, trying to see. Sawny narrowed her eyes.

There was a man in the storm, clearly struggling. Sawny couldn't see his features whatsoever, but he was tall and pulling a horse behind him, desperately trying to find shelter in the cave. The wind was blowing him from side to side, the rain hindering him immensely. Adriel was right; it had been wise to get out of the storm before it started.

"You're almost there!" Adriel yelled, surprising Sawny. She had almost expected him to pull out his sword. He usually assessed everything as a threat, but he continued to yell encouragement to the man, pushing him to come into the cave.

"Come on! Get out of the storm, come on!" Sawny yelled, joining in with Adriel.

The man stumbled a few more steps and met her eyes.

She could see him clearly now, see his black curly hair that was drenched because of the rain. He had a strong jawline and was wearing a white shirt and black pants that clung to him from the rain. Even from here, she could see the color of his eyes: green. The exact color of her own.

His eyes widened when he saw her face, a look of such shock and horror that Sawny took a step back. The man fell to his knees, releasing his horse, who took off running the other direction. Adriel glanced at her and then at the man and yelled something to her, but she couldn't hear him anymore. All of the sound had been drowned out except for the man's desperate and terrified shout.

"MARVIE!"

Chapter 5

Tenir, Orinth

18 years prior

"This is incredible," Marvie said, taking a long sip of the Orinthian wine and letting it trickle down her throat. "I truly can't understand how you found this place."

Sitting across from her, in a white shirt and pair of black pants, was Auden Frae. He was the most beautiful man that she had ever seen. From the moment she saw him, she knew she loved him. From his dark messy hair to his green eyes that normally held so much sadness. And his body, gods his body. He looked as if he had been sculpted by a master artist, all angles and sharp curves. She loved the way he looked tonight. Having not shaved in a few days, he had a scruffy beard that was just the right length. And his smile. She could die right then and there, and she would be happy, as long as she saw his smile.

She was so completely, entirely in love with this boy and she wondered if he had any idea of how much.

Auden shrugged and grinned. "I have my ways."

He had taken her out for dinner except it wasn't like a typical restaurant. It was outside and on a roof, with a perfect view of the city. He had gotten a table right at the edge of the building, allowing them to see it all. Tonight, the sky was an explosion of stars. The weather was warm and there was a gentle breeze.

They had been served fresh fruit, cheeses, and crackers before getting an incredible gourmet meal. They were now on the fourth course, which was a light and delicate soup, but Marvie was enjoying the Orinthian wine too much to stop drinking it. It was delicious and chilled to the perfect temperature.

"I love you," she said to him.

He smiled again. "I love you too. More than anything."

She shook her head. "Not more than I love you. I'm serious."

He rolled his eyes and laughed. "You're so stubborn, Marvolene. Just let me tell you I love you more."

"Never. Not in a million years."

It had been just over a year since they had fallen in love. It had been the best year of her life, filled with wonderful moments and memories with him. She couldn't see how it could get any better than this, getting to spend every day with the person who brought the most joy to her heart. She couldn't comprehend it. It felt too good to be true. It didn't matter to her that sometimes Auden had a look in his eyes of such sadness because she was helping him. That sadness, that darkness, went away when they were together. She was helping him to be whole again.

She couldn't wait for the chance to grow old with him. Just thinking about it made her heart race. Pretty soon, they were moving away from Tenir. They had talked about it already. Auden wanted to move back to Auntica with her. He wasn't attached to Orinth whatsoever, and once he had enough money, they would go. They would buy their own apartment and get to live out the rest of their days with each other. Maybe even have children of their own. She would be sad to leave her aunt and uncle, but they understood how much she adored this man. They were happy for her.

They were planning to get married in Tenir. They had decided to wait a little while longer before it actually happened. She was ridiculously excited for that as well. Marvolene Pere would become Marvolene Frae. It flowed perfectly.

"It's hard to beat Orinthian wine," Auden said, looking down at his glass that was empty once more.

"You can say that again." Marvie took another long sip of hers. "This is the nectar of the gods."

For the rest of the night, they ate and drank and talked and laughed and spoke of the future. They held hands across the table and didn't care if the whole world saw because they were in love and when you're in love, you don't care who sees. You don't care who judges. You only care about the person in front of you because they're the one who is going to bring you happiness and no one else.

They stayed on the rooftop restaurant for almost two hours, taking their time with each course and enjoying the moments they got to spend together. They saw each other almost every day without fail. Both had jobs but it didn't matter; they made time.

It was about midnight when they started to walk back to her home. Currently, she lived with her aunt and uncle in an apartment in Tenir and always tried to be back at a reasonable time. Of course, she often just stayed with Auden, but always tried to keep them informed on her whereabouts. Having lost her parents before she even learned to walk, her Aunt Sienna and Uncle Hewes had raised her as their own. They were never strict parents, allowing her to learn and grow on her terms. She never lost her Auntican accent, but was fluent in both Auntican and Orinthian. She had a good childhood and a good life; it had only become amazing when she met Auden.

They held hands, and Auden sang a song in Orinthian in his soft, sweet voice. Marvie laughed and sang along with him. Auden was from Orinth, she knew that much, but she had no idea about who he really was. He rarely talked about his past. She knew his father was alive, but his mother had died when he was very young. That was the extent of the details that he had disclosed to her. When she pushed him, he would close up and dodge the questions, so she tried to never bring it up. Still, she wondered often what had happened to him to give him so much darkness, so much pain in his eyes. She would never ask him. Whatever it was, it was in his past. Marvie was his future.

The streets were empty of people, surprisingly enough. Tenir was known for its vibrant nightlife and was normally crowded during this time. Marvie guessed they were lucky. The night was warm, there was a slight breeze, and it felt like they were the only two people in the world.

"I miss you already, Marvie," Auden said once he finished his song. "I miss you even when you're with me."

Marvie smiled at him. "But I'm right here!"

He shook his head. "Just the thought of having to leave you and walk home by myself makes me sad."

"My uncle and aunt have told you time and time again you can stay permanently. You would never have to worry then."

"I would still miss you. When you closed your eyes at night and fell asleep, I would miss you then. That's how much I love you, Marvolene. I would miss you when you're sleeping."

She squeezed his hand. "So, I'll never fall asleep then. How about that?"

He laughed. "I know how much you like to sleep so I wouldn't ask you to do that."

She nudged him with her shoulder. "You know me so well."

"I do, don't I? It's hard for me to fathom that it's only been a year. I feel like I've known you forever."

"What do you want?" Marvie snorted.

Auden grinned at her. "Nothing! Why do you ask?"

"Because you're being so ridiculously romantic and making me fall even more head over heels for you."

"I don't want anything, I swear. I'm just realizing how lucky I am to have you, Marvie, really. You saved my life."

"From what?" Marvie asked him.

"I can't even explain it."

She laughed. "You're crazy."

"Crazy for you."

She snorted. "Now you're actually being crazy," but her smile didn't leave her face.

Auden stopped suddenly and turned to her, taking her other hand in his own. His expression had turned serious. He took a deep breath. "Listen, Marvie, there's something I need to tell you," Auden said but before he could continue, an arrow whizzed past their heads.

At first, Marvie thought it was a large bird or bug, but then there was another one. She yelled and ducked.

"Run," Auden said, his voice suddenly taking on a tone of authority and seriousness.

Marvie listened. She took off running down the street, Auden on her tail as more arrows came towards them. Her instincts had taken over, but her thoughts were racing, trying to figure out what was happening to them. Were they being attacked by street thieves? What was going on?

She turned the corner towards her apartment when she was suddenly struck so hard in the head, she saw black. She didn't remember falling to the ground or laying there, she only remembered seeing double and hearing Auden, in a far-off muffled tone scream her name. She tried to respond, but her body wasn't listening to her brain. Everything had gone blurry and all she knew was the pain. She wasn't sure who had struck her or what they had struck her with, but it was severely painful.

"Marvie!" Auden screamed.

"Don't worry." The person in the shadows who had struck her stepped out. "It's not her we want to kill."

He was much older than either of them, probably nearing sixty, but still athletic. He had white, wispy hair on his head and wrinkled skin, but Auden couldn't help noticing the number of weapons he had on him. His entire waist held several knives, and two long swords were strapped to his back. In his hand was another sword, that *he had used the heel of to knock Marvie onto the ground. There she laid, Auden kneeling over her.*

"Who are you?" Auden growled.

"Do you ever wonder who attacks you at night?" It was a different voice this time, coming from behind. This man was younger and holding a bow and arrow. Still, Auden touched no weapon. He didn't need one. "And you were being so cautious too, weren't you? You were watching your back because we've been trying for years. But you got a little lazy, didn't you, Auden? You were up too late with your woman, a little too much wine, and here we are."

"Rookie mistake." A third and final man leaned against one of the buildings close to where they stood. He walked and took his position next to the first man. "A mistake that will cost you your life."

He had to get Marvie out of here. That was his priority. They said they didn't want to kill her, but that didn't mean they wouldn't. And he didn't want her to see what was about to happen.

"I don't know who you think you are," Auden said quietly, "but you're messing with the wrong person."

"Auden," Marvie murmured. He squeezed her hand. "I'm here," he whispered.

"This must be the lovely Miss Marvolene Pere. Yes, we know who she is. We've been watching you for a while, Auden Frae. Trying to find your weakness. And she's it," the first man laughed.

The man with the bow spoke to Marvie, "Marvolene, I'm sorry. You were never supposed to be a part of it. But your Auden? He's a bad man. He's dangerous to the future of Orinth and we would all be better if he were dead."

"Don't say a word to her," Auden said. He grasped her hand in his and used his other hand to check her pulse. It was weak, but it was there. She needed medical attention and fast.

"I'm going to give you one chance to get out of here before I kill all of you," Auden whispered. "One chance because this is the girl I love and I would rather not have to kill you in front of her. So, this is your one chance."

All three of the men laughed as the first spoke again, "You're untamed, Auden. You don't know how to use the powers you have. You don't even know who you are. We know who you are. We know how you got your powers, and we know what you're capable of. Did you know that you have the power to destroy this entire world?"

Auden's heart stopped, but he couldn't listen to them. Marvie was breathing faster and faster and starting to fade.

"No. Stop."

"That's right. I bet you don't even know who your real parents are, do you?"

"STOP IT!" Auden screamed but they continued laughing.

It coursed through his veins, overwhelmed his senses, and he was very frightened that if he exploded, it might somehow hurt Marvie. He didn't care if he died. According to these men, it may be better if he did, but Marvie had to stay alive. If Marvie was dead, there was nothing left. Marvie had to stay breathing and he needed to make her safe.

They moved like lightning, but he was faster. They charged at the same time, the man with the sword coming the closest. He had barely lifted the weapon when Auden lifted his own hands. The shadow consumed the man, quick as lightning. He screamed and dropped, only feet away from Marvie. The second and the third attacked simultaneously, but the shadow took them both faster, wrapping around them and choking every bit of life from their bodies. With a shudder and a shout, they fell too, next to their companion. It took all of ten seconds and three men were dead. The street was silent besides Marvie's labored breathing.

Auden didn't wait to see what happened, he scooped Marvie into his arms and took off running. She was saying something to him, but he couldn't hear because his head was pounding. He hadn't killed since he was fourteen and discovered he had the power by killing a boy named Conli. Since then, he had only used it to manipulate others but never kill. It was roaring with life beneath the surface of his skin, but he couldn't stop to calm himself down because he needed to get Marvie to safety.

He hoped to the gods she had been out when he killed them.

She still saw him as good. He absolutely did not see himself as good. He was the opposite of it. But when Marvie looked at him, he became good because he was everything she needed him to be and he would become whatever she wanted him to become.

The blood pounded in his head. How had they found him? He never knew who they were but since he had killed the first boy, people had attempted to take his life four or five times. The news about the killing had spread like wildfire; the boy who was dead with no wounds or injuries. Somehow, these people had tracked him down and wanted him dead, but he had outrun them. They hadn't struck in two years but somehow, they had found him when he was with the only person who mattered to him in the entire world: Marvolene Pere.

It seemed like hours before he reached her apartment. He ran up the stairs and pounded on the door, trying to hold back from screaming.

Her uncle opened the door.

"Auden? What happened?" His eyes widened with shock upon seeing his niece in his arms. She was drifting in and out of consciousness and talking with no understanding of the words coming out of her mouth. Her head, where she had been struck, was already swollen, a tiny drop of blood dripping from the wound.

"We were attacked on the way home," Auden said, pushing in and gently laying her on the sofa. "They hit her first. I didn't even see them coming." He was fighting to keep his voice from rising and panicking but it was hard not to. "We need a healer immediately."

Her uncle was already walking toward the door. "The healer is only a few doors down, I'll go get him." His voice held everything that Auden couldn't feel, mostly calmness. He had a cool head under pressure which was something Auden would never understand.

Marvie's aunt, Sienna, came running out of a room in the back. "Auden! What happened? Oh, Marvie darling!" she cried, kneeling next to the couch and observing the damage.

"She needs something to stop the bleeding," Auden said, ignoring the question and pulling Marvie's hair off the head wound. "Hurry."

Sienna didn't respond as she ran out of the room to collect it.

Auden held her hand. "I'm sorry, Marvie," he whispered.

Her eyes opened and darted around. "Why does it hurt so bad?" she whimpered.

He felt his heart break permanently right then and there. "It's going to be okay, I promise." If only there was a way he could keep that promise. With him around, there was no way.

"Auden!" she cried. "Auden, Auden!"

He leaned towards her. There was sweat covering her forehead and she was twitching severely. "I'm right here, darling. Right here."

"Don't leave me, please," she begged. "Please don't leave me."

"I'm right here, Marvie. I'm right here," he told her over and over until Sienna returned with bandages. She pressed them against her wound and Marvie cried out. Auden flinched at the noise; it shook him to his core. Sienna knelt down next to him, watching Marvie as she closed her eyes once more and stopped talking.

"What happened?" Sienna asked, panicked.

"We were attacked," Auden said, trying to hold it together. "We were attacked, and they hit Marvie before I could help her."

"Who attacked you?"

"I don't know," Auden admitted. "I don't know."

They were after him, is what he didn't say. Marvie had nothing to do with it. She was in the wrong place at the wrong time, because she had chosen the wrong person to fall in love with, and it had put her in danger. She could've died tonight. He always promised to keep her safe, but tonight he had done the exact opposite. He had almost gotten her killed. As he looked at her, the reality of it sunk in.

Her uncle returned with the healer and Auden left the room, leaving the healer to do her work. Her aunt and uncle stayed in the living room with her, watching every action done to their niece.

He sat at their dining room table.

It seemed like only days ago that they had all sat at that table, eating a dinner made by Marvie's aunt. They had talked and laughed and, eventually, played a game of cards. It made Auden feel like he had a real family. Later, Marvie and Sienna had left the room to take care of the dishes and Auden had asked him.

"Mr. Courtright, I know Marvie's father passed away when she was only little. Since that is the case, and you're the one who raised her, I figure you're the one I should tell my intentions."

Hewes Courtright was not a small man. In fact, he was rather the opposite. His shoulders were broad; he was muscular from years of working in construction. Although he was older and on the quiet side, he still intimidated Auden. He had no doubt the man would kick his ass if he ever hurt Marvie. At the moment, he leaned back in his chair, watching Auden with his dark brown eyes.

"And what are those intentions, Mr. Frae?" he asked him quietly.

"I intend to marry your niece, Mr. Courtright," Auden said, his voice shaking. He had imagined this moment in his head over and over again, but still, saying the words out loud filled him with such joy he felt as if he would burst. "I'm in love with her and I would do anything to protect her. I've been saving money for a long time and I have enough to provide for us. I'm asking for your blessing. It would mean the world to me—us."

Hewes had watched him for a second before his face melted into a smile. "I was wondering when you were going to ask me this, Auden. And it fills my heart with joy that you have. You're both young, but I've never seen such passion before. Of course you have my blessing. I never had a daughter of my own, but I was lucky enough to raise Marvie. She is a wonderful, special girl and I can't imagine a better man for her than you."

Auden felt, in that moment, he was going to cry tears of happiness.

And now, here he sat, alone. He hadn't asked Marvie yet. He had to tell her first, about his powers, about his darkness, about all of it. He couldn't let her tie herself to a man she didn't know the truth about. Tonight, he was going to tell her. Now, she laid in the living room, with a healer, because men had tried to attack Auden.

It seemed like a sign.

He loved her more than anything in the world, but being with him was dangerous. He, himself, was dangerous. But above all, loving him was dangerous.

He wasn't sure how long he sat there until Hewes himself came to get him.

"The healer just left," he said quietly, placing a hand on Auden's shoulder. "She's going to be okay. We're lucky it wasn't any worse."

"It's my fault," Auden said.

Hewes frowned. "No, Auden, it's not. Sienna and I both know you would do anything to protect Marvie. Tomorrow, we'll try to figure out who the men were and bring them to justice."

He had already taken care of that.

Auden stood up abruptly and walked back to where Marvie was laying. Sienna sat next to her but as he walked in, she stood. "I'll give you some time alone with her," she said quietly, placing a hand on his arm. "Don't blame yourself, Auden. Please. Marvie wouldn't want that."

He nodded and tried for a smile at the woman, but it wasn't even close. She left the room.

Auden knelt next to her. She was muttering in her sleep again, words he couldn't understand. There were bandages pressed to her wound still, but it had been cleansed, better than any one of them could have. Blood had stained her shirt, but she looked peaceful, somehow. Her blonde hair was spread on her pillow, making it look like she was wearing a crown. He grasped her hand.

He had to leave her.

There was no other choice.

If there was, he would find it, but there wasn't.

Love had to be unselfish.

The selfish thing for him to do was to stay with her, which he so desperately wanted to do. He could see it now. They would leave Tenir and go someplace else and have a house and a family and live out the rest of their days together in peace. If things were normal.

Normal people couldn't kill with their minds and normal people didn't have people attack them.

He loved her and because of it, he had to leave her.

"Marvolene Pere, I know you always get to say you love me more, but you're not awake right now, so I guess I get to say it. You saved my life. I love you more than anything in the entire world and because I love you, I have to protect you. And the only way I can protect you is to leave you. Go far away and make it so you can never find me because if you found me, I couldn't say no to you. I love you, but I promised to make you safe, and I can't do that. Dammit Marvie, if we were in a different place and I was someone else, maybe we'd have a shot. But I couldn't live with myself if I was the reason you were hurt. Even tonight is too much for me. So that's why I have to go."

Marvie didn't stir. Gently, he pressed a kiss to her forehead and squeezed her hand one more time.

"I love you," he said, a tear rolling down his cheek and falling onto her. "Please, please know I love you."

He stood up. He could hear Sienna and Hewes in the next room talking. He wanted to say goodbye to them too, but they would be able to convince him to stay. He couldn't. He had to go.

"I love you," he said one last time. Then, he walked out their front door.

By the next morning, he was on a horse, riding out of Tenir.

He looked back at the city, at its brick buildings, the sea sparkling on the horizon. This had become his home and now, he was leaving it.

"Auden Frae is gone," he whispered. "Goodbye, Auden Frae."

They knew his name. He couldn't be Auden Frae anymore because Auden Frae belonged with Marvolene Pere and that was impossible now.

He remembered a book he used to read at the orphanage, when he was young.

It was about a man who never died. No matter what he tried to do, he couldn't be killed. At first, he enjoyed it. Eternal life was something to celebrate, until he fell in love with a beautiful girl. It was wonderful, but while he stayed young, she aged and aged until she was dead and gone. The children they had together also aged until they died. He swore he would never fall in love again, because he kept losing the people he loved. Yet, a hundred years later, he fell in love for a second time. The process repeated itself. He decided to leave the continent and sail until he found a place with no people. He realized it was less painful to be by yourself than to watch the people you love die over and over again.

The man's name was Rider Grey.

"I'm Rider Grey," Auden said to himself, as he turned around and rode away from Tenir.

"My name is Rider Grey."

Chapter 6

The River Iyria

The stranger sat across from both of them, arms wrapped around himself, shivering. But the cold didn't seem to be bothering him as much as Sawny's face was. He hadn't stopped staring at it since he had screamed out the name of her...mother. This man knew her mother, but he hadn't been able to speak. Adriel had offered him a blanket, which he declined. Sawny offered him food and water, which he also declined. Instead, the man just stared.

Adriel turned to Sawny, shooting her a look that said *this isn't safe.*

His horse had run off and he had no supplies besides a knife strapped to him, and he hadn't said a word. For all they knew, he could be extremely dangerous. Why had he screamed her mother's name? There was a decent chance the reason wasn't good.

They had the same eyes. She realized that the moment he had gotten close enough for her to see. It didn't necessarily mean anything; there were lots of people in the world with green eyes, but something about it haunted Sawny.

"Can I have a word, Sawny?" Adriel said to her in Auntican. He was taking the gamble that this man only understood Orinthian.

Sawny turned around with him, backs facing the man.

"This is not a good idea," Adriel whispered furiously.

"Adriel, you were the one who yelled for him to come into the caves!" she exclaimed. "This was your idea!"

"I wasn't expecting him to scream the name of your deceased mother!" he said in reply, running a hand through his hair.

"He might have some answers for me."

"Or he might be dangerous."

"Either way…" Sawny said, glancing at the mouth of the cave. The water still poured down and every few minutes, thunder would shake the walls. The storm was just as intense as it had been and wasn't looking any better, "…we're stuck here. And you're welcome to send him back out into the storm if that's what you desire."

Adriel mumbled something under his breath she couldn't understand and then said, "Well, I'm not going to do that."

"Then it's settled. Just stay on your guard and we'll be fine." She put her hand on his arm. "I promise."

His eyes stared into hers before he gave a tight nod. "Fine," was all he said as they turned back to the man.

The stranger no longer looked terrified or shocked. Now, his facial expression was one of mild apprehension.

"You're not Marvie," he said slowly. The accent was clearly Orinthian, but he was speaking Auntican to her. Sawny noticed the slight tremble in his hands that he was trying to cover up. Whoever he was, he was quite adept at hiding what he was thinking. Besides the initial horror of course.

"No, I'm not," Sawny responded, not giving away any information yet. "Who are you?"

"I'm sorry for the imposition," he said, each word clearly pronounced and annunciated, as if he were struggling with the language.

"We can talk in Orinthian," Sawny said, switching over. "I know both."

"Thank you," he said, smiling a bit. "I never got the hang of speaking Auntican."

"Hopefully you'll understand the question better in Orinthian then: who are you?"

"You can understand why I wouldn't answer that question. Two strangers in a cave, in the middle of a storm."

"Two strangers who just saved your life," Adriel pointed out. It was true. After he had fallen to his knees, the man from the Wilds had run out into the storm and dragged him the rest of the way, sparing him from the downpour, the thunder, and the lightning. He had laid on the ground of the cave for a long time before dragging himself over to a wall and leaning against it, catching his breath. It was where he still sat, watching them both.

"I appreciate it," the stranger said, eyes not leaving Sawny. "I'm sorry for the wariness. You just remind me a lot of a person I used to know." He looked incredibly exhausted, with dark circles under his eyes, and his clothes were soaked and dirty.

"Marvie?" she asked.

"Yes. Marvie."

"Who was she to you?" she asked him, trying to pose as someone merely curious. "It seems to have upset you."

He ignored the question completely. "Where are you two going? It's unfortunate to be stuck in this storm."

Adriel raised an eyebrow. "What's it to you?"

He shrugged. "I figured only I would be crazy enough to be traveling to the Wilds during this war."

"Who says we're going to the Wilds?" Adriel asked him.

He smiled again. "I'm not going to hurt you, you know?" He used his hand to push his wet hair out of his face, continuing to shiver.

"Then tell us who you are," Sawny said.

He sighed. "My name is Rider Grey."

"What are you doing here?"

"I'm getting out of the rain."

Sawny made a face. "I mean why are you going to the Wilds."

"You got a question, now I get a question."

Sawny and Adriel exchanged glances. He gave her a short nod and she turned back to him. "Fine."

"Who are you?"

"My name is Sawny Lois, and this is Adriel."

He nodded. "I would say it's nice to meet you, but these aren't the best of circumstances, are they?"

Adriel asked, "Do you want a change of clothes, Rider Grey? Yours are soaked and it looks like your horse is gone."

Rider stood up and looked out the mouth of the cave. "I guess he is, isn't he? That is severely unfortunate," he said, his face staying straight. "Is there any chance he'll live through it?"

Adriel shrugged. "Horses are smart and resilient. There's a chance. But I'm from the Wilds. These storms are nasty. We're in a hurry, but even we stopped. I don't know how long it will last."

Rider put his head in his hands and said sarcastically, "Fantastic."

"So, the clothes?" Adriel asked tentatively.

Rider turned back to him. "Yes, please. Thank you."

Adriel walked towards his horse to grab the clothes as Sawny continued to observe the man. His sword was lacking. She noticed it right away. It wasn't the type of sword you would take on journeys. It was short and the handle was worn away. It looked like a long knife more than anything and Sawny struggled to come up with a reason why this man would bring it with him to the Wilds; a place that was notoriously violent.

Rider continued to watch the rain outside. "Why are you two going to the Wilds?" he asked, without looking at her.

"We're going to visit Adriel's family." The lie rolled off her tongue too easily. "We don't want to be here when the war explodes."

"Are you two married?"

"No."

"It's probably a good idea to get out of Orinth either way."

"What about you?" she asked him. She would find out every single detail about this man. She would find out where he was from and what his job was and if he had a family and why he knew her mother. She didn't care about the other things, but there were still so many questions she had about her past, about her true identity, about her real father. If she could figure out just some of those answers, or ways to find them, she would try. Rider Grey had looked traumatized when he saw her face. Obviously, her mother had been someone important to him. Maybe. It was hard to tell.

"I'm visiting a friend in the Wilds," Rider said.

"You're brave to be traveling alone," Sawny commented.

Rider shrugged. "I suppose."

"Especially with a sword like that."

Rider laughed a little. "Don't insult my sword. She may not look the part, but she gets the job done."

Sawny gave a small smile. "I'll take your word for it."

Adriel returned with his hands full of clothing and gave it to Rider. "I don't know if they will fit you," he said. They were about the same height, but Adriel was huskier than the Orinthian. "I gave you a couple things to try on and I'll take the things you don't wear back."

Rider nodded his thanks and turned around to change out of their sight.

As soon as he was out of ear shot, Adriel asked, "What did you find out?"

"Not much. He's here visiting a friend in the Wilds. Oh, and if he asks, we're up visiting your family."

"Did you ask about your mother?"

"No."

Adriel's eyes widened. "Sawny, why not? He could know something! About how she was killed or who she really was. He screamed her name. That has to be important."

Sawny let her head fall onto his chest. She had been enjoying their time together in the cave alone and was very disappointed to have it interrupted, especially by this man. "Maybe he screamed because he was the one to kill my mother, Adriel. We don't know if he's good. We can't trust him and just go out and ask him, because then he might try to hurt us too."

"Sawny, not to be insensitive, but self-defense is not really a problem for you anymore," he said, resting his chin on top of her.

She snorted. "I'm trying not to use it until I know I can use it properly. Everything I've used it for so far has been to kill people. Let's just try to get to the bottom of this without being too obvious."

"I don't understand you sometimes." Still, he wrapped his arms around her and pulled her close. "I do wish he hadn't come at the moment he did though," Adriel whispered in her ear, sending a shiver down her back. "Such terrible timing."

She hoped he couldn't see her blushing. "I agree," she managed to say.

Rider cleared his throat loudly and they broke apart. He had changed into one of Adriel's white shirts and a pair of grey pants that Adriel usually wore when they slept. He had combed his messy hair back with his fingers and looked a little less scrambled. "These will do," he said, handing the other clothes back to Adriel. "I appreciate it."

Adriel nodded. "It's not a problem."

Rider turned to Sawny. "Your horses are beautiful."

She beamed. "Thank you. Mine is the white one, Indira."

"That's a lovely name."

"I think so too. I'm sorry your horse ran away."

Rider sighed and looked outside the cave again. "Me too. I'm in a hurry to get to where I need to be, and I still have a while to go. I'm not exactly sure what I'm going to do now. Plus, that horse was a gift."

"What's his name?"

"Starlight."

Sawny cocked her head. "Starlight?"

He looked at the ground and a small smile lit up his face. "Yes, Starlight. My friend…my sister. My sister named him for me. It wasn't my choice."

"Is your sister Marvie?" she asked.

He looked at her, his face not betraying what he was thinking or feeling when she said the name out loud. "No. Not Marvie."

"Who is Marvie then?" She had just finished telling Adriel she didn't want to be obvious, but the innermost parts of her soul had to know. She was going to ask him straight up because she needed to know the truth. This person had possibly known her mother. Sawny hadn't met someone who had known her mother since the day she had died. Even if he had a slight connection to her, they could talk and reminisce about her. The thought of that filled her with a bittersweet joy. Yes, she would like that, talking with another person about her mother, Marvolene Pere. Sharing grief and memories.

"An old friend," he said, facial expression not changing. "Like I said, you look a lot like her."

"Yeah, I think I would."

That caused a reaction, but a small one. His face twitched. "What do you mean?"

She took a deep breath as she heard Adriel come up and stand next to her. "Well, she is my mother."

Rider's mouth opened and his face held even more shock than it had upon first seeing her. He said nothing for a moment, just stared before managing to get out, "Mother?"

Sawny nodded, biting her lip. "Yes. Marvolene Pere was my mother." She still wasn't used to the name. Sawny had known her mother as Ali Lois until she had read her last words, in the letter Jare had given her.

Rider's mouth closed. He turned away from her, walking towards the mouth of the cave and back, pacing. His hands had begun to tremble again, his face twitching at random intervals. He took long and deep breaths, probably intended to calm himself, before turning back to Sawny. "Is she still alive?" he asked, barely a whisper.

There was a slight jolt of pain in her chest, but she ignored it. "No. She died four years ago."

He stood in the same place, not even blinking. "How?" he asked. His face had taken on a mask of calm and that worried Sawny. The last time that she had felt calm was right before her power exploded and killed so many. Calm was what came before the storm and she had a feeling there was about to be a big storm.

Sawny chose not to answer the question. "How did you know my mother?" she said, this time with a little more demand in her voice.

"I told you," Rider said softly, his hands still shaking. "She's an old friend of mine."

"Did you know Auden Frae as well?"

It was like watching a crack in a foundation expand and expand until the whole thing came toppling down. Rider fell to his knees, letting out a sob and running both of his hands through his hair, tugging and pulling at it. Sawny took a step forward, her eyes beginning to fill with tears at the pure pain that was written across his face. She hadn't seen pain like that anywhere else except when she looked in the mirror at times. But this man? He looked like there was no happiness, no joy in the world. The rain and thunder echoed in the background, but she couldn't hear it anymore. Only his muffled cry.

"I," he began, staring up at Sawny with bloodshot eyes, "have not been called that name in a very long time."

She stopped.

She wobbled on her feet and was falling before Adriel caught her, helping her to sit down, saying something to her but she couldn't hear again. She could only see the man in front of her.

The man who had her eyes.

"You..." she whispered. "You're Auden Frae?"

He nodded. "I was. A long time ago. Not anymore."

Adriel was trying to support her and help her to stand up, saying, "Sawny, are you okay? Sawny?" but she was drowning in the past, in the memories, and everything that this meant.

Auden Frae was in front of her.

Rider Grey was Auden Frae.

Her father.

"Wait," he said, observing her reaction. His hands had stopped shaking but tears streamed down his face, falling like the rain outside their cave. "How old are you?" he asked.

Sawny could barely manage to answer his question. "I'm nineteen years old," she whispered.

"You—you're nineteen?"

She nodded.

She watched as the gears in his brain turned and he calculated it, because when he reached the conclusion, he seemed to choke. "It can't be true," he cried, to himself or to her, she couldn't tell.

Sawny's whole body felt as if it were about to break and if it weren't for Adriel, who was helping her to sit up, she would have fallen and laid there forever because this was him. Her father. Auden Frae. She didn't have to look for him because here he was, in a cave in the Wilds, in the middle of a dangerous storm. She had his eyes. This was the man that her mother had fallen so desperately in love with and who had walked away. For what reason, she didn't know, but in some way, this man had broken the woman who gave birth to her. All those days when she would lock herself in her room, and Sawny and Caleb would give her space, that was the reason. This man was the reason. And now, he knew the truth as well. He had a daughter who he had never known.

What would've happened if he stayed? She wondered. Her life would look much different than it did now.

"WHY?" Sawny didn't realize she was screaming the word at him until it echoed throughout the cave. "Why did you leave her?" She sounded close to hysteria and Adriel was trying to calm her down, but she pushed him back and stood up, marching over to where Rider or Auden or whoever he was sat. He had stumbled to his feet and held his hands up in surrender. She didn't realize she took a swing at him until her fist collided into a wall of power.

It sent shockwaves of pain up into her arm and she screamed, in anguish this time. Adriel shouted and went to move, but she could feel the shadow stop him. It wasn't coming from her though; it was coming from her father. He used the power to pin Adriel up to the other side of the cave, not intending to hurt him, but intending to protect himself. Adriel was about to attack him after just hearing Sawny yell.

She took a step back from Auden. "You have it too?"

His eyes, which were already looking crazy, widened. "I have what too?" he asked her, his hands remaining in their defensive position.

She could feel it in the air, the power that she herself possessed but it was different from hers. It was stronger, more experienced, less raw. It felt darker than hers, more malicious, as if it had festered for years and years.

"You have the shadow?" Auden asked, letting his hands fall to his side. Adriel collapsed onto the ground behind them and drew his sword, weakly, still dizzy from the slap of power.

"Adriel, it's alright," Sawny said, eyes not leaving her father's. "He won't hurt you again."

"I didn't mean to hurt you," Auden said apologetically. "It was self-defense. Sometimes it just happens."

"So, you do have the power?" Sawny asked him.

He nodded. "And I'm guessing you do as well?"

She nodded back to him. "Thanks to you."

His face had taken on a mask again, slowly apprehending the new information and the situation at hand. "She never told me," Auden whispered.

"Why did you leave?" Sawny asked, this time with less hostility in her voice. "You broke her, you know? She was never the same after you."

"I never wanted to hurt her," Auden said, choosing his words carefully. "But, as I'm sure you've figured out, being around someone with the power we have is dangerous."

"How so? Can't it be controlled?"

Auden nodded. "Yes. It takes a while to learn, but you can control it. It's difficult. The shadow is almost a living thing. It feeds on anger and hatred. The more people you control or manipulate or kill with it, the stronger it grows. Sometimes it takes on a life of its own. Like when Adriel tried to attack me, I was going to let him because right now I feel as if I deserve it. But the shadow didn't let that happen."

"Did you use the power on my mother? Is that why you had to leave?"

He shook his head. "No. Your mother, Marvie, was everything that was the opposite of the shadow. Kind and generous and happy and perfect. When I was with her, I was never even tempted to use it. It just kind of disappeared. I had to leave because there were people trying to kill me."

Adriel reappeared next to Sawny once more, not saying a word but scowling at Auden, who shot him an apologetic frown.

"Who was trying to kill you?"

Auden took a deep breath. "In order to explain that, I have to first explain a whole other thing. There are a lot of things I need to explain to you."

"So, start explaining," Sawny said.

"It's not that easy," Auden said.

"Why not?"

Auden gave her a look. "I just found out I had a daughter. There is a lot running through my mind right now."

Sawny laughed sarcastically. "And I just met the father that ruined my mother for the rest of her life. We're all suffering."

Auden said nothing, his mouth set into a straight grim line. He said nothing for a minute, letting the anger in Sawny fester until she thought she was going to explode. She didn't think the shadow would even work on her father though; it was apparent he was better trained and more powerful than she. Regardless, there was an anger in her unlike anything she had ever experienced, almost as strong as when she saw Adriel tied to the tree only days ago. This man was partly responsible for everything that had gone wrong in her life as well as her mother's. Yes, she was his daughter by blood, but he would never, ever be her father.

"When I was eighteen years old, and your mother was seventeen, we went out for dinner one night," Auden finally said, taking a deep breath. "We were celebrating being with one another for a year. It was a wonderful evening, perfect almost. Then, on our way back to her apartment, we were attacked by three men."

"I know about this," Sawny said. "She...told me. That was the night you left her. Why?"

"They wanted to kill me because of the power I had," Auden said. "I didn't know who they were. They knocked Marvie out. They told her that they were trying to protect Orinth. At the time, I had no idea how I was dangerous to an entire country. They tried to kill me, but they didn't even come close. I killed them with my power and then I rushed to get Marvie home. She was injured badly, and I was afraid she might die. She ended up being fine, besides a large bump on her head. But I wasn't fine."

"You see, her injury was temporary but the power I had within me would be there forever. I didn't know who the men were who tried to kill me, but being around me had almost gotten Marvie killed. I was a danger to her as well as myself. So, I left because I had to protect her. Sure enough, there have been several more attempts on my life since then. None of them ever worked, but at least she wasn't in any danger. That's why I left Marvie. I knew it might break her, because it broke me. But at least she would be alive."

They had found her, somehow. The men who had tried to kill Auden had tracked her mother down and killed her and Caleb. She couldn't fathom why. Maybe they thought Caleb was Auden. But either way, it was them. The group of people who wanted the man in front of her dead had killed her mother and father.

"It didn't help," was all Sawny said.

This time, it was apparent how the man was feeling. His face paled and his mouth fell open. "What are you talking about?"

"The men that tried to kill you found my mother and my father and killed them four years ago."

He swayed a little on his feet, struggling to stay standing. "What?"

"When I was fifteen years old, a group of seven men came to our home in Illias and slaughtered my mother and father. They died in my arms. My mother used her last words to tell me that you existed. And then she died, and it was because of you."

"Sawny..." Adriel said under his breath. But she didn't look at him or acknowledge him; she stared at the man in front of her, Auden Frae, her birth father. The reason why her mother was dead, the reason she was cursed with the powers she had. The reason for the pain and the suffering and all of it was because of him.

Auden stared back at her. "She died four years ago?" he asked.

She couldn't help herself; her power lashed out at him, wanting to make him feel some sort of pain for what he had put her mother through, what he had put her through.

Sawny flew back as his power slammed into hers, like a brick wall that was impenetrable. Adriel shouted her name as she landed flat on her back, her head slamming into the ground of the cave. She let out a soft cry as a jolt of pain coursed through her body. Her power didn't even come close to his and he hadn't even tried; it was his natural defense system. She was shocked by its essence and if she didn't hate him so much, she would ask him how. How had he become that powerful and how could she do it?

Adriel knelt down next to her. "Are you alright?" he asked, his eyes darting around, clearly panicked and so confused. She felt bad for him. He was in a bit of an awkward position.

She reached up and touched his cheek. "Yes, I'm fine. I'm sorry."

He shook his head. "Sawny, you need to take a few deep breaths before you do something that gets us both killed," he said quietly.

She glared at him. "Adriel, he is the reason for all of it."

Adriel raised an eyebrow. "Did he kill your parents?"

She protested. "No, but the people who were after him killed them. It's his fault."

"From my understanding of it, he did what he had to do to protect your mother. He left her and thought it would be the end of it. You think he would've left had he known you were alive? Do you think he would've left had he known the threat of the men was still there and only he could protect her? I know I don't know the whole story, but I can see his position from what he is telling us. Sawny, as much as I hate to say this, I think you need to give him a chance."

Sawny wanted to smack him for saying that but deep in her heart, she knew he was right. But instead of admitting that, she scowled at him some more and pushed him away, standing up by herself, turning back to Auden, who stood in the same position, observing them.

"I didn't do that. My power did. I would advise not trying anything of the sort anymore," he said sincerely.

"Your power is strong," was her only response.

He took a deep breath. "Sawny, there are some things you need to know. I didn't know you existed. I would never want to curse a child with the power I have, but there's more to it than that. And I know right now you hate me, and I understand why. I'll soon leave this place and never see you again, if you ask me. But there are things you need to know now."

She crossed her arms. "Tell me."

Auden glanced outside the cave. The rain continued to pour, but the thunder shakes had gotten few and far between. The worst part of the storm had passed and hopefully, it would be over soon. "As soon as the storm is finished, I must go."

"With what horse?" Sawny snorted.

He gave her a look. "I don't know. But where I'm going is time sensitive. It has to do with what I'm about to tell you."

"So, get on with it," she said, regretting the acid in her voice. Adriel was right; she needed to take a breath. It wasn't his fault that her parents were dead; she should blame the people that had killed them. Auden truly believed that leaving her mother would keep her safe and maybe he had been right. She had gotten fifteen beautiful years with her child and a man whom she loved. That might not have happened had he stayed with her. But she had already ruined any chance of a relationship with him, with her harsh words and quick judgments.

"My mother is the late Queen Natasha of Orinth."

It had been the last thing she had been expecting to hear. "What?"

Auden nodded. "Have you ever heard the term 'Last Heir' or 'True King'?" he asked her.

She felt her heart stop in her chest. "Yes," she whispered. "I know all about it. Why do you ask?"

"My mother, the queen, was the member of the Orinthian royal line to have the bastard child. I'm the True King. But I guess..." he took a long look at the outside of the cave, not being able to meet her eyes. "I didn't know you existed, Sawny. My child, my flesh and blood. It's a lot, to say the least. You have my blood."

Sawny took a step back, feeling all of her muscles slack at the same time. The world started spinning and she wasn't sure what was real and what wasn't. "Are you saying...?"

He finally met her eyes. "If you really are my daughter, then you're the True King, Sawny."

Chapter 7

The Wilds

Alida had never been to the Wilds before, and her first impression of the place was not exactly a good one.

Cold. That was her main feeling. Once they had crossed into the Wilds the temperature had dropped immensely. She was still in her drabby clothing from the inn in Tilda when, finally, Cassia gave her some new clothes. They weren't much better, a thin pair of pants and a white long sleeve shirt, also thin. The only thing that was semi-decent was the long coat she had given her, three sizes too big, but anything helped to keep the cold out. Alida wrapped it as tight as she possibly could around her.

The Wilds were beautiful; she had to give it that. Tall mountains covered in rolling trees, the smell of pine wafting in the air. There was so much nature but no sign of mankind. If she were here on a different occasion, she would've probably enjoyed the solitude. Since this place was to be the place of her death, however, she couldn't appreciate the vast open skies, the occasional sign of an animal, or the beauty. Instead, she kept her head down, not saying a word to anyone.

They ignored her, for the most part. Cassia sometimes found it necessary to chastise or tease her, but normally she left her alone. The guards spoke Auntican, with the occasional Orinthian conversation here or there. Alida was lucky; being fluent in both, she heard the things they said. They didn't know she understood them. She wouldn't let them know because it might come in handy at some point.

Cassia Messina stayed aloof from their camps when she wasn't bothering Alida. She would go for long walks and not return for hours. The guards would always nervously debate if someone should go after her. They didn't want her to be mad that they weren't more protective of her. On the other hand, they were also afraid of her anger if they were being overprotective and invading her privacy. One thing was apparent; they were all terrified of the woman. Alida had the sense to agree with them. A thousand years in the Shadow Realm would probably mess with someone's head. There was no denying it had with Cassia.

It terrified her even more that the guards were scared of her when they were so...unnatural. Every one of Cassia's men seemed to have endless strength, moved fast as lightning, and handled their weapons with a sort of ease Alida had never seen before. She had no doubt that Cassia had something to do with her men's seemingly elevated senses. How it worked and what was actually happening, Alida didn't know.

During the day, they would ride. Alida was always stuck in front of some guard the entire day until nightfall. Then, they would make a large fire and the men would drink and eat and talk. Alida would be tied up to some tree and most times, someone would bring her food. Then, she would be left there. Every night she tried desperately to escape, but the knots were tight.

She didn't know how much longer they had until the wall. The Wilds were vast, even after their land had been seized by Auntica and Orinth. Every day she braced herself to see it: the Shadow Wall. She didn't know what it looked like and had never once set eyes on it, but she had a feeling she would be able to tell. When she saw the wall, that would mean it was the day of her death. Every waking minute she had spent trying to come to terms with it, but she couldn't. There was no hope. No one was coming to save her and, even if they were, they had to take on a force of twenty abnormally powerful soldiers and a woman who had spent a thousand years in the Shadow Realm. It was a hopeless situation and Alida knew it.

She had regrets. A lot of them. But the biggest was Rider.

Her brother, Rider.

She forgave him. She didn't even have to think twice about it. She didn't know his reasoning for not telling her, but she trusted him and always had. Rider, the True King. When her death didn't open the wall, Cassia would know that he existed. Granted, she wouldn't know who he was or where he was, but she would search for him. Cassia was a patient woman. She would tear the world apart to find the person whose blood would open the Shadow Wall. But Rider was smart and resourceful. Hopefully, he would run. Hopefully, he would be smarter than Alida and manage to actually run, not be betrayed by two people she thought were her friends.

She had forgiven them too, Sahar and Roman. She didn't know why they had done it and did not believe it was justified in the slightest, but she wasn't going to die with hatred in her heart. Sahar was a complicated person. Roman was a Vacci, a notorious member of a gang who operated solely for the purpose of profit. Of course they would turn her in for money. They truly believed she was just a pawn in all of this, that Grafph would use her for a ransom. If they had known with certainty that she was going to die, Alida had to believe they wouldn't have betrayed her.

Maybe dying wouldn't be all that bad Alida thought to herself as she rode along on the horse of one of the soldiers. This was their fifth day of travel since they had left Tilda. They had to be getting close, but they weren't fast travelers. Cassia allowed them to stop for every meal. Alida, in an attempt to slow down her death as much as she possibly could, often asked to relieve herself, and she was granted that. It was clear Cassia wasn't in a rush. She could tell the woman was enjoying the trip. Alida could understand that. She had been in the real world for five years and before that, she had been in the Shadow Realm. Alida had to imagine that any sort of change of scenery was good for her, not that she cared. This was, after all, the woman who wanted to orchestrate her death, as well as the destruction of the entire world to bring back the man, or the demon, that she loved, Abdiah. She was dedicated, Alida would give her that. She couldn't imagine loving someone enough to wait a thousand years in a place of shadows for them. And then, destroy the world to bring them back. There wasn't anyone she would do that for.

Cassia always led the pack on her horse. Alida had to wonder if she knew at all where she was going. She hoped that she didn't because that would delay the inevitable. Occasionally, Cassia would jump off her horse, stare into the sky, murmur words to herself in a language Alida didn't understand, and then climb back up and lead the way. By the sideways glances the men cast each other, she could tell they were unsure as well. But they continued following her lead.

She saw Cassia stop once more and jump off her horse. She looked into the sky and pointed. "Storm clouds," she said to the guard next to her.

The guard whistled. "That's not good, m'lady. These storms in the Wilds can be rough."

"It's coming from the south. We should find cover then," Cassia said. "Are we anywhere close to a village?"

The guard shook his head. "No, m'lady. And even if we were, it wouldn't mean anything. These savages would try to kill us upon seeing us. We best find a cave or some other means of shelter until it passes."

Cassia sighed and her eyes met Alida's. She climbed back onto her horse and rode over to her. "You're lucky, Princess. You might have some more time in this world after all."

Alida smirked. "I'm so grateful," she said with a big, fake smile.

Cassia returned her smile with a wicked grin. "Don't get your hopes up. Once this is passed, we're only a day's journey away from the wall."

Alida said nothing. Cassia turned around and said to the guard, "Find us a cave."

They rode for fifteen minutes, the storm clouds rapidly approaching. Alida found it hilarious. Maybe she wouldn't be sacrificed to the Shadow Wall. Maybe instead, a giant Wilds killer storm would take her out. She would probably prefer that. Then again, just the thought of Cassia's face after she realized Alida was the wrong person made Alida laugh.

The guards finally beckoned them into a large cavern, large enough to fit twenty men, Cassia, and Alida. It wasn't large enough, however, to fit the horses of twenty-one people. The guard glanced at Cassia, who observed the situation with a straight face.

"What do we do, m'lady?" he asked her, voice quivering.

It was beginning to rain harder and harder and roaring shakes of thunder could be heard from the distance.

"There are a few trees right outside the cave that are large. Tie the horses to them and then come to the cave. The leaves of the tree will partially shelter them. If we lose a few, it's inevitable, but there's no other choice."

Alida was hastily thrown off her horse and into the arms of another guard on the ground, who marched her into the cave. Cassia followed them, brow furrowed at the unfortunate turn of events. The cave was large enough for them to be spaced out but still rather small. Regardless, it would keep them out of the storm. The guard sat Alida down at the back of the cave. Cassia looked over at her as the guard walked away.

"Do we need to tie you up or can I trust that you won't try to run again?"

Alida smiled at Cassia. "I would rather be thrown out into a storm a thousand times worse than this than have to spend another minute in your presence."

Cassia just laughed. "Well, don't worry, darling. You'll soon be rid of me when I slit your throat and let the blood fall onto the Shadow Wall." With that, she turned her back and returned to where most of the guards were standing, near the mouth of the cave.

For the next hour, it stormed, unlike anything Alida had ever experienced. The rain was a constant and each clap of thunder shook the cave in a way that made her terrified it might collapse. Every once in a while, she saw a lightning strike that lit the place up. The guards and Cassia watched the entire show, transfixed on the storm. Alida tried to close her eyes and sleep, but it was no use. It was loud. She could hear the panicked cry of the horses; that made her heart ache and made sleep an impossible dream.

Instead, she tried to picture better times than this.

She thought about her morning routine. How she rolled out of bed and stretched her muscles, waiting for Weylin to come in. She would walk to the window and stare at the view overlooking Abdul that never failed to stun her. Weylin would come in and bring her a cup of tea or hot chocolate and they would chat. She missed Weylin. Although they never became true friends, the girl had always been faithful to her. She knew without a doubt that Weylin would have her back through anything. After getting dressed, Alida ate breakfast. But occasionally, she met her father and Rider for breakfast on the balcony.

Those were the best of times. They would eat and chat and relax with one another. They did it often, but it was never not special to her. Some days, they barely said a word, exhausted from the previous day's excursion. Even in times of peace, there was so much pressure in running a country. Yet, even when they were tired, they were together. It put it all in perspective. Those were the times that really mattered, not the big memories, but the little ones.

She didn't know that she was eating with her father and her brother. Her family. And now it was gone.

There was something tragically beautiful about it.

What would she say if she ever saw either of them again?

It was ridiculous to even hope that would happen.

She had never been much of a spiritual person. The only time she went to the temple to pray to the gods was when it was required of her, on special occasions when the king and princess worshiped alongside their subjects. Only for publicity stunts. And even then, she didn't know what to say to them. The gods, according to their beliefs, were the group of people who had created the human realm and watched over them. It was simple enough. Be a good person, work to make the world a better place, pray to the gods and eventually, when you passed through the realms to get to the Beyond, you would be rewarded. If you didn't do that, then they would punish you. At one point in her life, Alida had known all the names of the gods and their various powers and stories. That was a long time ago and now she only knew them as an obscure group of people in the sky that she referred to as, well, the gods.

She whispered to herself, through the rain and thunder, "Hi."

"I don't know if you can hear me right now. Knowing my luck, you probably can't. And even if you could, you won't listen because I haven't done anything good in my life before. I'm not faithful and if I'm being honest with myself, I don't really believe you're there. Because if you were, then why am I here right now? But that's beside the point. If you're listening, please help me. There's so much I haven't been able to say. I didn't get to say the goodbyes I wanted to. I didn't expect to die and for what? I guess what I'm saying is save me. Please."

She spoke the last word with a choked sob.

It caught Cassia's attention, who turned and noticed her tears with a smile. She sauntered over, in her expensive-looking traveling clothes, and knelt in front of her.

"Is reality catching up with you, Alida?" she said mockingly.

Alida wiped the tears away and not being able to help herself, spat at the woman. A glob of her saliva landed on Cassia's cheek. "Have you ever read any stories, Cassia? Because there's one theme that recurs no matter what in those stories. Ugly bitches such as yourself always get their retribution. So, laugh right now, but I promise you that one day you are going to get what you deserve. It might be tomorrow or in a thousand years but, on my life, it will happen."

Cassia struck her in the face with the back of her hand faster than Alida could comprehend. She cried out and hit the ground with a thud. Her face was bleeding from the sharp rings the woman wore on her hand. Cassia knelt down and spoke directly into her ear, "Don't you dare talk to me like that you wicked brat," she growled, kicking her hard in the gut. "I spent a thousand years in a living nightmare so I'm not afraid of a little eighteen-year-old girl. It is you who should be afraid of me because I could make your life a lot worse than just killing you, you hear? I could put you through pain so intense it's indescribable. If I gave you even a hint of what I could do to you, you would wet your pants. Rest assured, your worst nightmare doesn't come close to what I'm capable of so do not EVER cross me again or I promise, you will regret it for the rest of your miserable life." She stood up and loomed over her. Alida had just managed to look up when she watched the woman's eyes turn pitch black.

She didn't even have time to scream as she suddenly experienced a pain unlike anything she had ever felt before. It wrapped itself around her and caused the most excruciating feeling. Her bones were all breaking at once, her skin burning, every hair on her head being pulled out. Her brain was exploding from the inside, trying to get out. She couldn't move, couldn't even struggle as the pain racked throughout her body. The shadow. Cassia was using the shadow. She was going to die. No one felt this pain and then lived to tell the tale of it. She tried to scream, but her lips wouldn't move and no sound would come out. All that existed was pain and nothing else.

And then it was gone, as quickly as it began. It released her body and she slumped onto the floor with a whimper. Her eyes were squeezed tight as the feeling remained. She heard the sound of Cassia's footsteps retreating towards the front of the cave.

It had been an agony unlike anything she had ever known.

Alida cradled her stomach, refusing to cry at the pain she felt. She could feel the blood dripping down her face from where the rings cut her, right below her left eye. It stung, but she refused to ask for help or to break down. No, Cassia would not win. Alida wasn't even scared of her. Go ahead and try it. Try to make her life a nightmare because she did that well enough on her own.

She didn't know how long she laid on the ground, not moving, feeling the effects of the shadow before a guard came over and lifted her to her feet. He dragged her outside the cave, back towards where the horses had been tied up. The storm had passed, with minimal damage, it looked like. Most of the horses were still tied to the trees, though jittery. Alida was having a hard time seeing and let the guard do all the work as he lifted her onto the horse and climbed up behind her. Then, they were off again, without a word. Cassia led, without even a glance at Alida.

Besides fallen trees and branches, the storm hadn't affected the journey. They had been traveling on an old path that had been abandoned by the people of the Wilds and it was unharmed. Alida didn't know if she could feel any worse than she already did. She lifted a hand to her face and wiped away a mess of blood. No, it definitely could've been worse. Stay positive, Lida. She heard Rider's voice in her head.

The sun was beginning to set, though, so only hours after their break in the cave, Cassia called for them to make a camp. Alida was ripped off the horse once again and hastily tied to a tree. The guards weren't as gentle as they normally were. This particular guard pinned her arms behind her around the tree and tied the rope so tight that it cut into her wrists. She bit the inside of her cheek to keep from crying out. Cassia was watching and she didn't dare give her the satisfaction of watching her be in pain. He left her when he was convinced the ropes were tight enough and returned to the camp. This time, she was farther away from them, which she was thankful for. She didn't like to be in the midst of their gatherings, their binge drinking and eating that Cassia allowed them. They had built their bonfire in a small clearing and were preparing for what looked to be a large celebration. Alida wasn't surprised. This would probably be their last night on the road.

They had tied Alida up a little distance away but still close enough to watch her. Not a single one did, however. Most were too preoccupied with the coming ordeal. Cassia also seemed to be involved in the preparation. She had something to celebrate; killing Alida the next day. Every few minutes, Cassia would shoot her a smug grin and return to what she was doing. Instead of buying into it, Alida let her head fall onto the tree behind her and closed her eyes. She ignored the physical pain and mental anguish and tried to focus on more happy memories. Dancing in Rein with Ellis. She almost smiled at the memory of the boy with curly blonde hair and a goofy smile. She should've just stayed with him. She should have permanently become Nova Grey and hid in Rein, right under everyone's nose. She should've bought that dress in the dress shop. She shouldn't have gotten on that boat and befriended Sahar and Roman.

But wasn't that what life was? A series of should haves and could haves? A series of what we would have done if we had a second chance, but we don't so this is our life? Spending the rest of your days wondering what could've been if you did something different? Of course, Alida would go back and change some things, but who wouldn't? Her decisions and her choices had led her here and there was nothing she could do to change it.

She was eighteen years old and she had tried to live every moment to the fullest. Maybe she had and maybe she hadn't. It didn't seem to matter anymore.

She was hovering on the line between sleep and reality when a hand clamped over her mouth. Every bone in her body froze. Not a single guard had approached her since she had been tied here. She would have seen someone go behind her so whose hand was on her right now? She opened her mouth to scream when a voice whispered furiously in her ear.

"If you want to live, you need to do everything I'm about to tell you."

She didn't recognize it whatsoever, but it was distinctly male and deep. She closed her mouth and nodded once, eyes watching where Cassia stood, talking and flirting with one of her guards.

"I'm going to untie this rope. Are you strong enough to stand?" The hand left her mouth.

"Yes," she whispered in response, wondering what in the world was happening.

"Stay seated with your hands in the exact same position until I say the word, okay? Timing has to be perfect."

"Who are you?" Alida asked.

"I'm here to make sure you don't die. It doesn't matter who I am."

"Fine," Alida said, her heart racing. She said nothing but felt as he cut away ropes, being careful to avoid her wrists. He observed it for a moment.

"They tied it pretty tight, didn't they?" he mumbled. She didn't answer.

Finally, the rope fell down, easing the burden on her wrists. She sighed in relief and avoided the urge to immediately shake her arms loose, but she didn't. She stayed in the exact same position as he had asked her too. She didn't know who he was. She didn't know if he was on her side or if he wanted her for the same reason Cassia did. But it didn't matter. This was an opportunity for escape. With Cassia, there was none. So, she would go with him and take her chances.

"There's going to be a distraction soon," he said to her, kneeling behind her ear but still staying out of sight. "That's when we move."

"The woman," Alida managed to get out, "she's dangerous."

He scoffed, "Well, of course she is. Cassia Messina, right?"

"What…how? How do you know that?"

"We've been following you soon after you left Tilda," he said.

"Who are you?" Alida asked again.

"The Society of the True King," he whispered.

"What?" Alida said. The group of people who attempted to kill the True King to protect the world. The people who Cassia claimed had been a constant thorn in her side. "How is that even possible?"

But the man was gone. Alida tried to turn her head, but it was too much of an effort to do so. She was so tired. She felt as if she hadn't slept in ages. Her entire body still ached with the feeling of the shadow, a phantom pain traveling throughout her body. Alida wanted sleep, and was sure she would drop without it, but right now, she was escaping. She had to be alert. The guards were unaware of anything going on. They were too focused on the giant deer roasting above the fire and the drinks that were being passed around. Cassia hadn't looked at her since she had earned the attention of one of the young guards. Alida fought to keep from gagging at the sight. Here she was about to kill Alida to try and open the wall for Abdiah and she couldn't manage to keep her hands off one guard. But right now, it was helping.

Suddenly, from the opposite side of the clearing was an explosion. It lit up the dark night as all the guards sprang to their feet. Something was on fire, but it was hard for Alida to see or hear what was going on. She was drifting in and out of consciousness, the pain starting to grow. Something was searing the inside of her brain, burning and twisting. She couldn't help herself this time; she screamed.

Cassia was staring straight at her and Alida realized it was happening again. The pain became worse, running up and down her body, through her bones, inside of her head and she screamed and quivered as she couldn't keep herself upright. She fell to the ground, shaking. The world went dark and the agony grew. It shattered her world. There was no past, present, or future, there was only pain.

And then it was gone. Alida slumped onto the ground, unable to move.

She felt a pair of arms scoop her up and take off running. The person was talking to her, but she couldn't hear through the ringing in her ears. She was not doing her part very well, she thought with a bitter feeling. All she was supposed to do was listen to what the mysterious voice, the Society of the True King, had said and she had failed. It didn't matter though. She wanted to die now. The anguish was too much, and it would be easier if she stopped breathing and died.

Alida wasn't sure how long she was in their arms until she was set upon another horse. She prayed to the gods that it wasn't one of Cassia's guards. But last time she had prayed to the gods she got slapped in the face, kicked in the gut, and then tortured with the shadow. She should probably stop doing that.

They rode for a long time, not stopping once. Alida hated to admit it but she had to pee and she was hungry and she was tired and wanted nothing more than to climb into a bed and fall asleep forever, but she couldn't raise her voice to speak.

Now she knew why Rider hated his shadow. He was capable of things like that. She had never felt anything like it and couldn't fathom wielding that sort of power, carrying that burden. Rider had used it to kill before and she couldn't imagine his guilt.

The horse stopped. The person behind her jumped off and helped her down, again scooping her into his arms. He carried her a few steps and then she heard a door open. A door? How? Weren't they in the Wilds? She felt as her body was set onto a soft cot and she relaxed into it, keeping her eyes closed. She didn't want to know who had her. She didn't want to know if she was a captive or if she was free. She just wanted to sleep.

"What happened?" a voice asked in Orinthian, but in an accent she had never heard before.

"She was fine when we found her. Then Cassia used some sort of power on her to cause her pain. It was horrifying. She's been in and out since."

She felt a pair of cold hands grasp her head. "It will do nothing permanent. She needs rest."

Alida sighed in relief. Well, thank the gods for that at least, she thought as she finally let herself drift into a dark sleep.

She wasn't sure how long she slept. She dreamed about Sahar's boat, The Valley. She dreamed she was on it, standing on the top deck, looking at the stars on the River Dela. She dreamed that she was free. That none of this was going on and the world was normal, and she could go about her life without worrying about this or that. She dreamed Rider was there with her, staring up at the skies, but it was the Rider who wasn't the True King. It was the Rider who was just her brother and nothing else. Somewhere, her father was there but she couldn't see him. She couldn't take her gaze off the stars.

Then, she opened her eyes.

She was staring at the top of some sort of hut. The roof was made of wood and it was small and warm, and she was comfy. There were thick, wool blankets layered on top of her and she felt like a child again. The aroma of meat was wafting from somewhere she couldn't see. Besides the cot she was laying on, there was a shelf with books and bottles of something, and a table next to her. She tried to sit up, but her head still ached. The pain remained there, albeit numb, but there.

She tried to call out, but her throat was dry. She didn't know where she was. Was this just another prison? It was comfier than her last one, but a prison was a prison. Someone had changed her into different clothes, a black shirt and black pants. Her hair was braided into two ponytails. She felt it with her hands. She hadn't done that. Since being captured by Cassia she hadn't cared at all about her physical appearance. Alida reached up and touched her face. There was a bandage on where Cassia had cut her. Someone had tended to her and well, but who?

She sat up again, this time successfully. Right as she did, the door opened. A woman stepped in and closed it behind her, looking at Alida. Alida froze. She had never seen the woman before in her life, but she was sure she was from the Wilds.

She was older, probably as old as her father, with wrinkled skin and long black hair that almost reached her waist. Her clothes were beautiful and colorful, and Alida couldn't take her eyes off them.

"How are you feeling?" the woman asked, walking towards the cot.

"I feel better," Alida responded. "But who are you? And where am I? And who saved me and am I still in danger?"

The woman smiled. "Genuine questions. My name is Kal. It's the best I can translate into your language. You're in a village in the Wilds, temporarily."

"How?"

"We've had an agreement with the Society of the True King for a long time."

"The Society. They're the people who have been trying to kill the True King for the last thousand years." At least according to Cassia.

Her smile faded. "No, not kill. The Society of the True King wants to avoid death. If the sacrifice is made and the wall opens, we will all die. We're trying to protect the world. The True King is a threat to the world. One death to spare many others."

Alida wisely didn't mention she knew who the True King was and instead nodded. "I see. And they saved me, why?"

"I told you, Princess, their goal is to avoid death. You are not the True King. Cassia Messina was going to kill you, even though you weren't. It was our duty to save you."

"I appreciate it," Alida said. "Truly, thank you."

The woman, Kal, laughed. "Don't thank me. You're an Orinthian. No offense, but I don't care if you live or die. It was our leader who saved you."

Alida chuckled, slightly uncomfortable. "To be clear, I'm Orinthian who has no hatred whatsoever towards people of the Wilds. That's an old prejudice that our society has long forgotten."

Kal burst into laughter. "Okay, Princess, whatever you say. You're leaving soon. Join us for dinner and then you'll be on your way."

"On my way where?" she asked.

Kal shrugged. "I'm not sure. Wherever he tells you to go, I'm guessing. Cassia Messina will not be far behind you."

"Who is he?" Alida asked.

"I'll let you find out for yourself, my dear." Kal offered her hand and Alida took it, despite her earlier comments about not caring if she was dead or not. Her head was filled with a sharp pain in protest, but she swallowed it down. She needed to eat.

The village in the Wilds was small, only a few huts scattered in a clearing. There were almost no people around the village, but Alida occasionally saw faces pop up in windows. The people of the Wilds were terrified, and it saddened her heart to see it. Kal led her towards a fire. It gave her chills, thinking of the fires Cassia's men used to make, but she reminded herself that she wasn't their captive anymore. She was now the Society of the True King's captive, whatever that meant.

It was a small group of men, of all different races and ages. There were about ten in total, sitting around the fire talking quietly. Kal cleared her throat as they approached the group of men. Alida shivered.

"She's awake," Kal said to them.

Their faces rose to meet hers, but she stared at her feet. Alida didn't know if they would harm her or not and the thought of it terrified her. One of the men stood up and turned to them.

"Thank you, Kal," he said in Orinthian. "You're free to go, if you choose."

Kal let go of her arm and said, "It was nice meeting you, Princess Alida. I doubt we'll meet again." With that, she walked back towards the smattering of huts.

Alida looked up into the face of a man.

He had to be older than her but not by much. He had dark hair that was messy and eyes that were a cross between gray and blue. He was tall, but with a small, strong frame, and had a face with traces of a beard on it. The man was clothed in a plain white shirt and gray pants and was observing Alida.

"You're looking better than the last time I saw you," he said to her.

She recognized the voice. It was the one who had untied her. "Thank you," she said, unable to recognize her own throaty voice. "Thank you," she said again.

"It's not a big deal," he said. "I'm glad we got there in time, before she had the chance to kill you."

"It wouldn't have worked anyway."

"It would've been quite a waste, wouldn't it?" he replied, sounding amused. The men behind him laughed quietly.

"I have some questions."

"I imagined you might." He pointed towards an empty bench by the fire, across from where he was sitting, "Take a seat. We're eating shortly and until then, you can question me to your heart's content."

Alida shivered a little and the man raised his eyebrow. "Someone get her a jacket," he said. She began to protest but before she could even try, a jacket was wrapped around her shoulders. She thanked the person and sat down on the bench, not taking her eyes off the man.

"Who are you?" was the first thing she asked.

"My name is Caellum Asher," he said. "I'm the leader of the Society of the True King. As was my father before me and his father before him."

So, it was true. The group of men who had saved her was the Society of the True King, the group of men whom Cassia had described as a thorn in her side because they were constantly trying to track down who they believed to be the True King and kill them. They must've known, then, that it wasn't Alida. No one had ever tried to kill her before. Except Cassia, and Alida had a strong suspicion that the woman had known she didn't have Arca's blood. She just wanted death because she enjoyed it.

"What is the Society of the True King?" Alida asked, compiling all of her thoughts into a question.

"Initially, we were a group trying to figure out who truly was the Last Heir. I'm assuming you know what that is?" Upon her nod, he continued, "That person is known as the True King. After we finally found out, we realized the world would be safer without the blood of Arca. So, it became our duty to protect the world by finding and killing the True King."

Alida raised an eyebrow. "Regardless of who that person is? Regardless of whether they have a family or friends or a life here?"

Caellum stared at her. "Yes. Regardless of that, Princess, because by one person sacrificing that, then we can all focus on having a family and friends and a life here. Do you understand that if the True King ever fell into the wrong hands, it would be over? The moment their blood even touches the wall, it disappears. The barrier between us and an entire world full of people like Cassia is gone. They are free to come into our world and terrorize us and who here can stop them? No one can. I hate death. I hate killing. We saved you because we knew you were innocent. But the one life I won't preserve is that of the True King."

Alida said nothing for the moment, but looked around at the faces of his men, who were nodding in agreement. "Do you know who the True King is?"

Caellum exchanged glances with one of his other men before responding. "Yes. We do. We've known for a long time, but we've lost him more than once. We've never been able to kill him, he's always managed to slip away. My father almost had him once, but it didn't work. I took over for my father."

"How many of you are there?"

"Dozens and growing by the day. Some of us, like this group here, exist solely for the purpose of saving lives and killing the True King-" Alida almost laughed at the irony of his statement, "-while others focus more on research. Checking and double checking to make sure we have the right person. Because, like I said, our main purpose is to protect innocent lives. We don't try to kill someone unless they're completely and utterly guilty."

"Of what?" Alida exclaimed. "Of being born to the wrong family? Of having the wrong mother and father and ending up in a situation they didn't ask for?"

Caellum didn't blink. "You think that the True King is completely innocent?"

She pretended to think about it and ponder before nodding. "Yes, I do. I think the True King is probably a good person who was born in a situation he didn't ask for. Does he deserve to die because of it? No, not at all."

"Tell me, Princess, have you ever heard of mysterious mass killings in which men's bodies cannot be burned after they are dead?"

Oh Caellum, she thought, you have no idea how much I have heard of such mysterious killings, so much to the point I feel as if I may have been the reason for some of those mysterious killings. "Once or twice," Alida said instead.

"The only people who are capable of that are people cursed with the shadow. And we have reason to believe that only the True King has the shadow. There have been rumors that more people possibly have it, but it's not true. Only Arca's heir has the shadow, so that means that those killings were done by the True King. He has killed before, multiple different times. Doesn't he deserve to die for that?"

Alida leaned forward, placing her arms on her knees. "That's not the question you should be asking though, Mr. Caellum Ashton."

"Asher," he said with a hint of a smile on his face.

"Asher. The question you should be asking is do you deserve the right to decide whether he should live or die?"

He pondered this for a while. "It's a good point, Princess. It is. But I'm not going to stand here and debate the ethics of what we do."

Alida snorted. "Weren't you just trying to convince me it was ethical for you to kill one life to possibly save multiple others?"

Caellum stood up as a woman approached the fire with a tray. "We saved your life, Alida Goulding. I don't think I have to convince you of anything." The men laughed at this as he thanked the woman and took the tray from her, opening it up to reveal multiple sandwiches. Caelum passed them around by throwing them across the air, to the smiling faces of the rest of the Society members. Alida's ethics debate had been forgotten entirely. She crossed her arms and leaned back. At least she wasn't with Cassia Messina. She wasn't sure what these people wanted with her or where they were going. But she was relatively sure she wasn't going to die soon.

Except they wanted to kill Rider. That terrified her. Caellum had said they knew who the True King was. Their purpose was to kill the True King, no matter how he tried to justify it. Rider was constantly in danger. She didn't remember any incidents from her childhood of people trying to kill him or harm him in any way, or her mother, who had also been the True King. Nothing made sense to her anymore.

Caellum tossed her a sandwich and she caught it. She took a small bite and realized just how hungry she was. It was roast beef and cheese, she believed, but at this point, she didn't care. Cassia hadn't been very concerned about her nourishment and this had been the most food she had gotten in days. She ate it gladly.

As soon as she had taken her last bite, Caellum said, "Alright, we need to get moving. We rode far enough away and backtracked enough that I don't think she'll be able to find us, but we can't take any chances. Let's go."

Alida stood up, waiting for someone to explain what was going to happen to her. Was she now stuck in this small village of the Wilds? That thought frightened her. From talking to Kal, it was clear Orinthians, especially their princess, weren't exactly popular. Although it seemed like the Society and the village had an agreement and got along, Alida was unsure if that extended to her as well.

The men had disappeared somewhere as Caellum approached her. "You never did ask what exactly happens now, did you?"

She shrugged. "I guess I should."

"It's not safe to be alone in the Wilds, even in this village. They have an agreement with us because they want the True King gone just as much as we do. But I don't know how they would react if we left you here. We can take you back to Tilda and figure out what comes next."

"They're still going to be looking for me. Cassia Messina will be. I won't be safe in Orinth either. It was a pair of Orinthians who turned me in in the first place."

"I don't think you have to worry about that anymore. Trust me."

"Well, that's the thing, Caellum," she said. "I don't trust you. I don't trust anyone."

Caellum looked at her. "That's probably for the best," he said, before turning around and walking towards where the rest of the men had gone.

With a long, deep, labored breath, she followed him.

Chapter 8

The Wilds

He was gone.

Adriel was gone.

Two months after she had met him in her apartment, traveled the continent with him, fought to save his life over and over again, and realized she was falling for him, he had left.

Sawny didn't know why she was so shocked by it; of course he would leave. Why would someone like Adriel ever stay with someone like her? She was a mess. That was a confirmed fact. When they first met, she had been a mess. Now, on top of all of it, her powers, her killing, her father she didn't know until hours ago, and the fact it was HER blood that could open the Shadow Wall.

Not Auden's.

Not Alida Goulding's.

Hers. Sawny's.

It hadn't taken Adriel long to figure out that if Auden was the True King, it was he who had killed his brother.

Auden had admitted to it.

Adriel had stood, strangely calm, if not a little dazed, and asked him why.

He had done it to protect the princess, Auden had said. He had done it to protect his kingdom. Adriel's brother had kidnapped a child. There was no telling what he might do.

Adriel had stood very very still.

He had drawn his sword and whispered, "I don't want to do this. But I made an oath to my tribe. I made an oath to my brother. I have to kill you." And although it was probably the worst idea in the entire world, he charged at the man who had killed seven men with his mind and possessed a power so strong and evil that it could destroy the world.

It wasn't Auden's power that threw Adriel across the cave.

It was Sawny's.

She didn't even realize what she was doing as she threw her hands out, but she wasn't going to let Adriel kill her father, kill the man her mother had loved. She wasn't going to let him kill the man who had sacrificed everything; a life with his lover, happiness, and a future, all to protect Marvie. She had her own range of complicated feelings towards him that she hadn't even begun to process, but letting him die was not a part of the plan. She unleashed a part of her power.

Adriel flew across the cave as Sawny had only minutes before and hit the wall and the ground with a large crash. Sawny cried out and reached toward him but stopped. She had just done that. Subconsciously, her power had protected Auden.

Adriel had managed to stand, his eyes wide and shocked at the events that had just taken place.

Sawny herself wasn't sure what had just happened. She glanced across at Auden, who stood frozen in place, staring at her.

"Sawny," Adriel said breathlessly. "What did you just do?" he asked, his voice cracking.

Her heart was breaking. Who was she kidding, it was already broken and had been for a while. She had been fooling herself to think she could ever make it whole again. Some people were permanently broken, and she was one of them.

"You can't kill him, Adriel," she said softly.

Adriel staggered back, as if he had been punched in the gut. "Sawny, you know I have to. I made the oath to my tribe. I—I've been waiting for this moment for as long as I can remember."

"Adriel, he is my father," Sawny yelled at him. He stared at her, no traces of the man she had come to know in front of her. Instead, it was her enemy, a person of the Wilds. She hadn't meant to yell at him. She was confused and frightened. Her blood could open the wall and her father had killed Adriel's brother. She was the True King. "You can't kill him because no matter what he has done, he is my father. Can't you see that?"

The rain had stopped as had the thunder, and a long, bitter silence had filled the void in the cave. Adriel had taken the reins of his horse and a step towards the mouth of the cave. "No, I can't see that. He killed my brother, Sawny. I can't go home until he's dead. I have nowhere else to go."

She would have rather endured being hit with the pain of the shadow a hundred times over than watch him as she spoke her next words. "There's nothing else I can do. I'm not going to let you kill him."

He stumbled back, out of the cave, eyes not leaving hers, He shook his head and turned around. Without a word, he mounted his horse, kicked it in the side, and began to ride. Sawny took a step forward and reached toward him, as if to stop him. Before she knew it, he was out of her sight. He was gone. He was out of her life, possibly forever. Only hours ago, they had shared a passionate kiss and now? He had vanished into the cold air of the Wilds.

Sawny wiped a tear from her face. Gone. Adriel was gone.

She turned back to Auden, who watched her, expressionless.

"Don't say anything," she warned him.

"I wasn't planning on it," he replied. "You didn't have to do that. He wouldn't have come close to me, and I wouldn't have killed him."

Sawny mumbled, "Didn't I just say to not say anything?"

"Thank you, Sawny."

"I didn't do it for you. I don't think my mother would appreciate me letting my father die only an hour after meeting him for the first time."

"What now?" Auden asked her.

She stopped. What now? Her case was technically solved, wasn't it? By luck or by chance, they had stumbled across the man who had killed Adriel's brother. She had found him. No, she hadn't. He had found them. Either way, Adriel was her client no longer. According to their contract, he owed her a large amount of money, but she had a feeling he wouldn't pay up. She should've run after him and demanded her money, but she didn't. What now? It was a question she didn't know how to answer. But the princess was still in danger. That, for the moment, had to be her goal.

"We weren't going to see Adriel's family," Sawny admitted.

Auden raised an eyebrow and gave a small smile. "I kind of figured that. Where were you going?"

"We were going to stop Grafph from killing Alida Goulding."

The smile dropped from his face. "Why?"

Sawny shrugged. "I knew it wasn't her whose blood would open the wall. I just had this gut feeling I couldn't let her die. Adriel…" It made her chest pang to say his name. There was a raw pain that had settled into place, but it hadn't quite sunk in that he was gone. "Adriel agreed to help me."

"I was on my way to do the exact same thing."

"What was your reason?"

Auden took a deep breath. "I told you my mother, and your grandmother, was Queen Natasha, who died only a few years ago, which makes Alida my half-sister. And I suppose it makes her your half-aunt? I don't know if that's a real thing."

"The eighteen-year-old princess of Orinth is…my aunt?"

Auden smiled a little again. "It's very strange."

She had to agree. "You've got that right."

"It explains why you felt the need to come rescue her. She's your blood. It was a gut instinct and I'm glad you followed it."

"Then let's get going," Sawny said.

"What about Adriel?"

There was a throb in her heart. "He doesn't matter right now. We have to go get the princess."

"We'll have to keep an eye out. He wants to kill me. There's no telling where he might be waiting to get a jump on me," Auden said.

Sawny ran a hand through her hair. The last thing she could imagine was seeing Adriel kill the man who stood before her, her father. But Auden was right. Adriel had made an oath and it was clear he would do anything to fulfill that oath. They would have to keep an eye out for him.

But in reality, it was one warrior against two people who had demonic killing powers, just by outstretching a hand. They wouldn't have to worry too much about it.

"Do we take your horse? Mine's gone," Auden asked, interrupting her thoughts.

Sawny glanced back at Indira, who still stood in the back of the cave. At least she had her horse, if nothing or no one else. "Indira is strong. She can carry us both. Do you know where we're going?"

"I do."

"Then let's go."

Sawny walked to Indira and stroked her before starting towards the mouth of the cave.

Auden held up a hand to stop her. "Let me check to make sure it's all clear." Without waiting for an answer, he ducked out of the cave and disappeared. Sawny closed her eyes and leaned into Indira. She was the True King. It echoed throughout her head and very being. True King. A month ago, she didn't know what it meant. Gods, a week ago, it was a word that she had read in a dusty book in a library.

Now, it was her identity.

Auden stepped back in and nodded at her to follow. She led Indira outside and glanced around. There was no sign of the man from the Wilds or anyone else for that matter. Sawny climbed on her horse's back and motioned at Auden. Without saying a word, he lifted himself onto the back. Sawny kicked Indira's side and then, they were off.

It was chilly, but the humidity from the rain had warmed it up slightly. Auden told her vaguely what direction they should be heading but other than that, he didn't speak. Her body language probably wasn't great right now. She wished she could speak to him, ask him about her mother, ask about his life, tell him about her own. She had a bad knee-jerk reaction. It wasn't her father's fault that her life had come to this. In fact, a part of her was unbelievably happy to meet someone who had loved her mother, someone who would understand the grief. Auden hadn't been aware that she was dead. Maybe that was why he was so quiet. He had found out in the last hour he had a daughter, who was the True King, and the love of his life had been murdered, probably because of him. It was a lot to process.

But she understood how he was feeling because the last week had shaken her world to the core, the most since her parents had died four years ago. In the last seven days, she had found out the identity of her birth father and her mother's story about how they had been in love. She had found out that she possessed a power that came from beyond the Shadow Wall and could destroy people with her mind, among other things. Some part of her was demon. And to top it all off, she had found her real father, been informed that he was the True King, and had passed his blood onto her, making her the True King. It was her blood that would open the wall. She was the person Grafph wanted. It was too much and what she really needed was a week to lay in her bed, in her apartment, and process it.

She was glad they were going to save the princess because at least that would distract her. It would put her time and energy towards something important and then afterward, who knew what would happen? Auden had said a group of people had tried to kill him because of his power, but even he wasn't aware of her existence. So how could that same group of people know? She was still safe. After she saved the princess, she was done with this. All of it. She would go back to Illias and pick up right where she had left off with her business. If Auden wanted to follow her in an attempt to have something of a relationship? Well, they would have to talk about it. But one thing was for certain; she wasn't a part of this war. As long as she stayed hidden, she would keep the whole entire world safe. Whatever happened to Orinth and Auntica during the fight was irrelevant.

Her power was a distraction. Even now, riding on Indira towards the Shadow Wall, she could feel it. It was a constant in all of this, the low simmer of the shadow, whispering to her to let it go. Let go of her hold on it. Let it explode and who cares what it destroyed? It would make her feel better, it told her.

She concluded, in that moment, her life would never be the same.

It terrified her.

Adriel had promised he wasn't going to leave her and look what had happened. He had broken his promise. He had left.

She had begun to fall for him, and now, he was gone.

It didn't matter anyways. No one wants something that's broken, and Adriel was no exception.

Though, she thought that the reason they had advanced to where they were was because a part of him was broken too. His brother had ruined him. He had spent his life cleaning up a mistake that wasn't his. He faced the risk of exile if he didn't kill Auden. On top of that, Adriel was a man from the Wilds and exposed to the constant and unrelenting prejudice against him. He had been beaten and tortured for it, and if it weren't for Sawny, he would have been killed for it. Adriel was broken, in his own way, although he never showed it.

Except when she had defended her father.

When he stumbled back, she had seen it in his eyes. The pain. The shattered part of him that could never be fixed because you can never change the past. She saw all of it in that instant and prayed to the gods that one day he could heal.

She hoped she wouldn't see him again; hoped he wouldn't attempt ambushing them because she would still protect her father. She was partly responsible for his exile now. He would hate the sight of her, but what did it matter anymore? Just one more person in her life who had left it. This time, it was Adriel's choice.

She pushed those thoughts out of her brain as a tear streamed out of the corner of her eye. Sawny couldn't afford to think like that right before she might be going into battle. She didn't know what to expect when they reached the princess. Together, her father and she were a force to be reckoned with. Of course, Auden was more experienced and so much more powerful, but she had the shadow too. They didn't have to worry about fighting in the traditional sense.

Grafph would probably be accompanied by soldiers. He would have a security detail. But waves and waves of men, she had figured out, were nothing compared to her power. Their power.

It terrified her but, in another sense, it was thrilling, the things she was capable of.

It also scared her that she would be going so close to the wall. She was tempting fate. There she was: the girl whose blood could destroy the wall. No one knew besides Auden and Adriel but still. It just seemed like a disaster waiting to happen. She was almost tempted, right there and then, to turn the horse around and ride back to Illias and pretend like none of it had happened. How had she benefited from this trip? At first it had been for the money and then it had been for Adriel, but both of those things were gone. She supposed she did have the friendship of Matahali and that was powerful. It seemed like ages ago that the forest witch had possessed her mind and forced her to relive her greatest trauma, the murder of her parents. It was almost ironic, she had relived the moment her mother had confessed the identity of her true father and now, said father was riding on the back of her horse.

Besides Matahali's friendship, this trip had broken her on a level she couldn't quite comprehend yet.

"Are you okay?" Auden said in her ear, almost if on cue.

"I'm fine," Sawny replied, an obvious lie.

"This is all a lot for me too, Sawny," he said.

"I know. And I'm sorry that I blamed you for what happened to my mother."

"You were right though. I shouldn't have left her."

"You did it to protect her."

"And now look where she is."

"She got fifteen years with her daughter and husband," Sawny replied to him. She had briefly explained to Auden about who Caleb was. "Who knows what would've happened if you hadn't left."

"I would've gotten to see my daughter grow up," Auden said in a faraway voice.

"I'm here now. And I don't know what exactly is going to happen, but we'll figure it out." Sawny wished she felt as confident as she spoke. She had no idea how they would figure it out. Absolutely none. She was lost on all levels at the moment but reassuring her father that it would work out. What in the world was going on?

"You said you lived in Illias?"

"My whole life. The outskirts of Illias with my mother and father. And then once they died, I moved into the city. I used all that I had to buy an apartment and I've been living there ever since."

"What do you do?" he asked.

"I'm an investigator of sorts. I have my own business. I track people down, figure things out, stuff like that." She chuckled a little, "I realized I had a knack for it when I was searching for you, actually."

"That sounds interesting," he replied.

"It is. I get a lot of strange cases. Adriel hired me to find the man who killed his brother."

"Congratulations."

Sawny had to laugh at this, bitterly. "It doesn't help. I don't think he's going to pay me anymore."

Auden said nothing so she asked him, "What about you? Where did you go after you left Tenir?"

"I went to Abdul. I had always been told that I had been born there. I changed my name to Rider Grey and did the same thing I did in Tenir; just got by. It was around that time when my father found me, somehow. I don't know how he did it. I don't even know who named me Auden Frae. It wasn't my mother or father. However, he did it, he found me. I knew him, of course. He had visited me in the orphanage from time to time, but he decided to tell me the truth then. That's when I found out my mother was Natasha, the late queen of Orinth."

"It took me a while to work up the nerve, but I managed to contact her. She knew who I was the moment she set her eyes on me. She asked what my name was, and I told her Rider Grey. I left Auden Frae in the past, with Marvie. My mother and her husband decided to let me live in the castle, just to be close to them. I would be a low-level servant to avoid suspicion. Even after she had become queen, the threat of the story of the bastard child coming out would still harm her. They asked me not to tell Alida and I never did."

"When Alida was kidnapped and I killed those men, that's when they promoted me to advisor. That's what I've been doing ever since. I love it. I get to be around my family and do something that helps others. I finally feel like I found my calling. The only thing that could possibly make it better is Marvie. But she's gone, and I would've never been able to go back to her, so I've made the best of it."

Sawny didn't speak for a while, letting it all sink in, until finally saying, "I'm glad you found something that made you happy."

Auden smiled a little. "I can't wait for you to meet Alida. She's my closest friend. I love her," he snorted, "like a sister. She is my sister."

Sawny couldn't imagine meeting the princess of Orinth in person. She was Auntican. She was supposed to hate these people, but she couldn't because they were her family.

"I hope I get the chance," Sawny said in reply.

"Me too," Auden said, smile fading. "Me too."

They were silent for the rest of the ride, but their brief conversation had managed to lift Sawny's spirits, just a little. They had nineteen years of life to catch up on. Nineteen years of experiences that they had missed out on together. Not that Sawny didn't appreciate Caleb. Auden hadn't witnessed her first steps, but Caleb had. Caleb had taught her how to shoot a bow, to defend herself, to survive. Caleb was her father, but Auden was her father too, and every moment that fathers dreamed of had already passed.

"How did you learn to use the shadow so well?" Sawny asked him, trying not to think out on the missed time or regrets or any of it. "Did someone teach you?"

"No, I just learned. I wouldn't say I use it well. I know what I'm doing but it's not exactly a great thing to know. I found out I had the shadow when I was fourteen. I killed a boy who was about to hurt me. After that, I realized that I could use it to manipulate people. It became a habit. I didn't stop until I met Marvie. By then, I was experienced."

"I still don't know everything about it," he continued. "When Adriel tried to attack me and the force sort of threw him backwards, or when you tried to punch me, and it did the same to you. It's never done that before."

"I'm sorry about that," Sawny chuckled nervously. "There was a lot going through my head."

Auden laughed. "I forgive you. I'm sorry my power lashed out. Like I said, I didn't try to do that. The shadow, it adapts. It grows. It changes. It's never the same for me. It's terrifying. It's almost like I have someone else controlling me."

"I know what you mean," Sawny said. "My power, it awoke almost a week ago. A group of Orinthians attacked Adriel, beat him up and tortured him. They were about to kill me when I just exploded. I didn't even know what was happening. It just felt like my anger had manifested into a force. I could control it, but at the same time, I felt like it was controlling me."

Auden nodded. "Exactly."

"It's terrifying."

"I know."

"It's even worse to think about being the True King," Sawny breathed.

"I'm sorry. I'm so sorry," Auden replied, with genuine sorrow in his voice.

"It's not your fault."

"I wouldn't wish it upon my worst enemy, Sawny. When Natasha told me that it was my blood that could open the wall, I went back to my room and threw up. Just the knowledge that I had the power to destroy the world, it was too much. But when she told me, she was wrong. You were already alive at that point."

"I have to ask you a question. I'm not trying to cause a fight or blame you for anything. I truly just want to know."

Auden took a deep breath, "Right. What is it?"

"If you would've known my mother was pregnant, would you have stayed?"

He was quiet for a long time before finally answering, "Without even a question, Sawny. You have to understand. If Marvie would have been conscious, I probably wouldn't have gone. If her aunt and uncle would've said one thing to me, I wouldn't have gone. It wouldn't have taken that much to convince me to stay. I thought I was doing the right thing by leaving. I thought I was protecting her. But the chance to be a father, the chance to raise a child of my own? I guess I threw it all away when I left. And the worst part is I didn't even know until today."

Sawny didn't say anything in response. It hurt her heart to hear him talk like that. She felt extremely guilty, now, for the way she had initially treated him.

She tried for humor. "You're, what, thirty-six years old? It's not too late to have another child," she laughed, but it was forced.

Auden laughed mercifully. "Maybe. I won't ever love anyone the way I loved Marvie."

"She was amazing," Sawny agreed.

"I wish I would've gotten to see her one more time. And Sawny, when we get to Alida, regardless of what happens after, I promise you this; I will find the people who killed her and make them pay. I don't know if it's related to me or not, but they won't get away with it."

"I've tried since the day they died. But you're welcome to as well."

"I don't think I could live with myself if she died because of me."

"Auden, I think I should probably tell you this. The reason I know your name and the reason I know you left my mother is because she sent me a letter. She left it with Sienna, and it somehow got back to me. In the letter, she told me I should find you and then let you read it."

Sawny stopped Indira. They had already been riding for hours and her horse could use a break. It was like Adriel had told her; it was no use arriving to save the princess with no energy left. If they took a brief break and recharged, they had a better chance at accomplishing their mission. And she could show him the letter.

They both jumped off the horse, Auden waiting with one eyebrow raised. With a deep breath, she reached into her pocket and pulled out the letter she had been carrying. She handed it to him and then pulled some food out of Indira's bag, trying to distract herself. What she really wanted to do was watch his reaction to her mother's last words to her, the letter where she admitted she had never stopped loving Auden.

He didn't take his eyes off the paper for a long time. He said nothing, but tears streamed down his face. Sawny couldn't help but watch him. Her mother had been right. She could see it in him. A part of him was broken. A part of him was dark, but she understood it now. How could you not be broken, with the burden that they bore? Was that how the world saw her? Broken, a part of her always lingering in the darkness?

Finally, Auden handed the letter back to her. "Thank you for letting me read that," he whispered. "I know it's personal, but thank you."

"I've had four years to cope with my mother's passing. I'm not over it, but I hope that can provide you with a little closure. Knowing that she still loved you, even at the end."

"It does," was all he said in return. Sawny handed him a package of dried fruit and he ate it without comment. Together, they got back on the horse and continued.

"What made you fall in love with my mother?" Sawny asked him. "How did you know?"

Asking about her mother was distracting her from the gaping hole in her heart. Adriel was gone.

"I knew it from the moment I saw her," Auden said, a hint of a smile on his lips. "It wasn't like a magical moment, where the world just stopped, and it was just us. It wasn't anything overly dramatic or what you read in the stories. She just walked into the shop where I worked, and I saw her, and I just knew. I felt like I had met her before. Who knows, maybe I had. Maybe it wasn't the first time our souls had found one another. I know it's ridiculous, but I just knew."

"It's not ridiculous," Sawny said.

"Maybe not."

Sawny wanted to switch the subject. Her stomach was starting to hurt. Adriel was gone.

He had walked away.

She couldn't have let him do what he wanted to. He was going to kill Auden. He was going to kill her father who she had just met. He was going to kill her flesh and blood. How could she have allowed him to do that and live with herself after? Even if she had, Auden would've stopped him with his power. Adriel knew that and still had pulled out the sword and attacked. He was thinking of only his mission and his oath to his tribe. She couldn't understand why that stupid oath even existed. Regardless, Adriel had put the oath over Sawny. He had chosen it instead of choosing her.

"I'm not going to leave you."

She thought that he'd let the oath go. She thought he had given up on finding the killer, or at least killing the killer. But he hadn't.

"I promise."

She laughed bitterly at that broken promise.

"Stop the horse," Auden commanded, and she didn't think twice about tugging on Indira's reins to stop her.

"What's wrong?" Sawny asked.

Auden jumped off the horse and stared. They were back to being in a forest. It wasn't thick by any means, but Sawny could see it would only get thicker. On the horizon, she could see mountains rising into the sky. They had arrived: the Wilds. It was beautiful and extremely cold. She took a deep breath, recalling that this was the place where Adriel had grown up. But of course it was. It was rugged, dangerous terrain. Where else could he grow up but here?

"There are people coming," Auden whispered.

Sawny jumped off Indira and stood next to him. She saw nothing but trees and more trees. "I don't see them."

"I can feel something," Auden said.

"The shadow?"

"Yes and no. I've never met someone else with the shadow until you. When you used your power, I could feel it."

Sawny nodded. "I felt the same."

"Right now, I can feel someone else's power. It's not good. It feels...old. Deadly."

Sawny closed her eyes and tried to feel it, but she couldn't. "How far away are they?"

"Not far. We should find somewhere to hide."

Together, they led Indira behind a thicket of small trees, blocking them from the sight of anyone who would approach from the north. Someone else with the shadow? She thought they didn't exist, but Auden had felt it. An old and deadly power. That didn't sound good. But they both had the power. They both had methods of defending themselves. Hopefully, the person would pass by and not see them. It had been days since she found out about the princess going to be sacrificed. They were cutting it close by stopping. Alida could already be dead.

Sawny bit down on her lip from yelling as the ground started to shake. A large group of horsemen rode into the clearing, soldiers by the looks of it. They wore neither Auntican nor Orinthian clothing, but black clothes. It was hard to tell where the men were from. They were large and serious-looking. Sawny shivered.

Leading them was a woman in a white cloak on a white horse. She had long, blonde hair that flowed behind her as she rode, proudly, sticking her chin out as if she owned the land she was riding on. There was something about the woman that set Sawny's teeth on edge, but she couldn't figure out why. Auden sucked in a breath. "That's her," he whispered to Sawny. "That's where the power is coming from."

As if on cue, the woman stopped her horse.

The men behind her stopped immediately, as if they were used to her frequent pauses. She took a deep breath through the nose, closing her eyes.

Sawny froze. Now, she could feel it. The woman's power flowing through the air. It hit her like a stab to the heart and she tried not to gasp at the magnitude of it. Auden had been right. It was deadly. She could feel the hatred, the malice, and the depth of it. And the age. It was older than Sawny, older than Auden, older than these countries and these people. It frightened her. Who was this woman and how had she come to possess something so evil?

The woman opened her eyes and had a sour expression on her face. "She's not here," she said. "They're already back in Orinth. We're days behind them." She sounded almost bored.

"Should we just give up, m'lady?" said the horseman closest to her.

The woman turned to him, eyes glowing. "I told you already. It's not about the wall anymore. I want to see the Orinthian bitch die and I want to do it myself. I've waited a thousand years and I can wait longer if it means I get to kill her. No one, not even the princess of Orinth, gets away from me." She held up a piece of ripped cloth. "I can find her using this piece of her shirt. She can't get very far. It'll only take a week at the most, we'll bring her back and kill her. And then go from there."

"But m'lady. She said it herself, she's not the one we need. Why waste our time? Let's start to track the real one."

The woman didn't move her hands, but her expression darkened and Sawny suddenly felt the power in the air, and she had a hard time not audibly gasping. The man who spoke began to shake. Suddenly, he fell off the horse and dropped to the ground, beginning to convulse. He started to scream; a shriek filled with so much pain. His eyes rolled into the back of his head and continued to shake. Sawny grabbed onto one of the small trees to keep herself upright. Her power had never felt like this. This was something different. Auden barely moved, barely even breathed, and she knew he felt the same.

She wasn't sure how long they watched the man quiver on the ground before his body finally went still. Sawny put a hand over her mouth to keep from shouting out.

The woman turned to the remaining men, whose faces held utter shock and fear. "Does anyone else want to add to this conversation?"

All of them, every single one out of the twenty or so, shook their heads, eyes not leaving the corpse of their fallen comrade. The woman smiled, something so wicked and atrocious that Sawny had a hard time not gagging at the sight of it, along with the corpse.

"Good," the woman said, climbing back onto her horse, smile not fading. "Then let's keep going." Without another word they began to ride. Sawny didn't move until they were completely out of sight.

She let out a breath and shook her head. "I...I have no words."

Auden stepped out of the bushes without responding and looked after the group, still partially out of sight. After a few moments, he turned back to her. "They're gone." He walked towards the body of the man and kneeled next to it. He pressed his fingers onto the man's neck and looked back up. "He's dead."

Sawny took a few steps forward, guiding Indira out of the brush, "Was that normal? Is that what we're capable of?"

She watched as Auden closed the man's eyes and stood back up. "Somewhat. We can kill and cause pain like that. But I've never seen nor felt anything quite as powerful as what she just did. Terrible, evil, power."

"That was awful," Sawny agreed. "Who was that woman?"

Auden shook his head. "I don't know. I've never seen her before in my life, but I could feel it. She's dangerous. And she's the one who's trying to destroy the wall it sounds like, not Grafph. I have no idea."

"It sounded like she's using her power to track Alida right now."

Auden nodded, and a small smile appeared on his face. "So, Alida escaped."

Sawny sighed in relief. "It appears so. But she's still in a lot of danger if that woman wants to kill her. What do we do?"

Auden turned to look at Sawny. "Well, Alida is safe for the moment, at least. If you want, Sawny, you can go back to Auntica. That woman is trying to destroy the Shadow Wall and the person she needs to do it is you. Being close to her is dangerous, even if she doesn't know who you are. I'm going to go find Alida. I'm going to follow that woman and try to get to her before she does. Then, I'll figure out who the woman is and what we need to do to stop her. But it might be best for you to go."

Sawny took a deep breath. The thought of going home was more appealing than anything. Back to her apartment in Illias, to her own bed, her own bath. No more sleeping on the ground, shivering in the cold, wondering what problem they would have next. Home to her cases and the somewhat normal life she once had. She would be safe there, away from the madness that had come into her life. She would just be Sawny Lois again. Even better, the questions that had haunted her were answered. She knew who her real father was. She didn't know who had killed her parents, but she did know Auden would find them and kill them. Sawny could go home.

But so much had changed since then. She had changed since then. She knew about her powers and who she really was. She had grown in the months since she had been gone. Before Adriel had showed up in her apartment, she was constantly crumbling, hating the world for what had happened to her parents, for what had happened to her. Now, Sawny knew that the bad that she had gone through was not meant to define her; it was meant to drive her into finding the person she was supposed to be. She didn't know who that was yet, but she was on her way to finding out. But to stop, go back to the way things had been before? She wasn't sure she could. It was safer to go back, yet something told her she couldn't.

"I want to stay," Sawny said. "I'm in this now. I've been through too much to not see this through. I'll go with you to find Alida. Once we find her and make sure she's safe, I'll go back to Auntica."

Auden nodded but she noticed his slight smile. "I'm glad," he said. "I am."

"Me too," Sawny said, returning his smile. "Me too."

Chapter 9

Outskirts of Tilda, Orinth

The memory of the pain was as fresh as if it had just happened.

She hadn't slept since, which didn't make a lot of sense, considering how exhausted she was. But every time Alida closed her eyes, she could feel it, the pain that Cassia had given her. It felt as if every bone in her body was breaking simultaneously, every organ shutting down, every fiber of her being on fire, an intense, excruciating anguish. The mental suffering was almost as bad. In that moment, all the good had been sucked from her world. Rider was dead. Her father was dead. She saw the corpses of Sahar and Roman and every person she had met on her journey. The wall was open, the demons had been unleashed, and Orinth had fallen. There was no hope left.

It was hard to close her eyes without seeing that.

Sleep wouldn't come.

She had been traveling with the Society of the True King, the people who had tried to kill Rider. She didn't tell them she knew that, but a part of her realized that these people, Caellum and his men, weren't bad. They believed that what they were doing was right. Maybe, in a way, it was. They thought by killing one life, they were saving the world. Never mind that the one life they needed to kill was the life of her brother, the one person who had been her constant companion and friend who had saved her life. The Society men were kind to her, always asking if she needed anything and if she were comfortable. It was a welcome change compared to the way she was treated by Cassia's men. She always tried to match their level of politeness, but it was growing difficult to even bother.

When Rider had used the shadow on her at the castle, the effect had worn off immediately. He had manipulated her mind using his power and then it had stopped. This felt strangely permanent, as if Cassia had marked her. The memory of the pain was almost as agonizing as the pain was itself.

She had been given a sleeping roll as well as her own bag of supplies with a hunting knife and small sword. She was being treated as an equal, not a prisoner, which she was grateful for. By a miracle of the gods, she had the picture of Rider. It was almost ripped in half, faded, dirty, and waterlogged, but she still had it. She couldn't look at it anymore without feeling desperately sad.

It had been two nights since the Society had rescued her from Cassia. They were in Orinth, that much she knew. They had set up their own camp around a small fire, but Alida kept her distance. She stayed close enough to be safe but far enough away to have her own space. She heard them in the evening, talking, laughing, and eating. A man ended up bringing her a plate of fresh and seasoned venison, which she didn't touch. She felt hungry, but every time she tried to eat, she inevitably threw up.

And now, she laid on the ground, where she could hear the loud snores of the men. Every time she closed her eyes, she felt the pain even more.

Alida bit her lip and slid out of her bedroll. She put on a cloak that she had been given and started walking, taking deep breaths of the fresh air. A nice walk would do her good. A nice walk would make her tired and get her some damned sleep. If that didn't work, she would have to ask someone just to knock her out. That would work, right?

She stopped right before she was about to step off a cliff. She gasped; she had barely noticed the sharp fall onto a grassy field below. Her eyes followed where the field led, and she saw it: Tilda, Orinth. They were on the upper part of it, about a hundred feet above the plain. The lights of Tilda sparkled from afar. She had to guess they were about four or five miles out. It was a strangely peaceful sight, being on the edge of a fall and watching the city. It was quiet out and she could almost imagine that she was the only one in the world and that none of what had happened in the last month had actually happened. With a sigh, she sat down on the ground, hugging her knees to her chest.

"It's a beautiful view, isn't it?"

Caellum had come up behind her, standing with his arms crossed, shivering. He wore only a white shirt and a pair of black pants. His dark hair looked like it had been slept on, but the bags under his eyes told her he hadn't gotten a lot of it.

"Aren't you cold?" she asked him.

Caellum hadn't spoken to her much on the journey. In fact, none of them had spoken to her much. They regarded her like a piece of fine jewelry they were transporting, being utterly careful. She wasn't sure if she was happy about it or sad. On the one hand, it made her feel lonely, but on the other, the last time she had befriended a group of people, they turned her in for a ransom.

He shrugged. "A little." His gray eyes gazed across at the city. "This is it. My favorite spot in all of Orinth."

Alida followed his stare. "Are you from Tilda?" she asked him.

"Yes, I am. Born and raised. We always try to camp here, at this spot, whenever we're traveling. Just so I can look from right here. I see you found it, too."

"I couldn't sleep," Alida said.

"You haven't been able to for a while, have you?" he asked her.

"How do you know that?"

"I've seen you wander out and about at night a few times. I don't sleep well either," he said.

"It's been difficult," Alida admitted.

"I'm sorry," Caellum said. "I wish there was something I could do to help. I'm sorry we didn't get there quick enough to stop her from hurting you."

"No, don't blame yourself. It's thanks to you I'm alive, Caellum." She glanced at him.

"You can call me Cael, Princess. Everyone does. Caellum makes me think I'm being scolded by my mother," he said with a smile. Alida smiled back at him. He had a goofy, boy-ish smile that made his eyes light up and she thought it was cute.

"Alright, Cael," she said. "You can call me Alida. Princess makes me think I'm being scolded by my father."

He laughed at that. "You weren't what I imagined you would be," he said to her.

"What does that mean?" Alida asked him.

"I'm twenty years old and have grown up and lived in Orinth my entire life. Of course, I've heard of Princess Alida Goulding. How couldn't I? I've heard she has long hair, but when I found you, you have short hair. I've heard she never leaves the castle without a security detail, but when I find you, you're by yourself and in the hands of a thousand-year-old demon-human lady. I've heard that the princess won't do anything that'll make her break a nail and then I come to find out you ran away from the castle to protect your kingdom, tried to sail away to

Nagaye, got captured, and fought to escape over and over again. Most of the things I've heard, I suppose, aren't true."

Alida laughed. "No, I suppose they aren't, are they? And, for the record, I still try not to break any nails."

Cael sat down next to her as she asked him, "Have you heard any news about the war?"

With everything that had happened, she had almost forgotten about the fight between Auntica and Orinth. For Alida, it had become everyone versus Cassia Messina. They all needed to band together to fight the woman who wanted to destroy the world. The last she had heard of the war, Orinth had just won the first battle on the border between the two countries. Since then, not a word, but to be fair, it had been a busy couple of days.

"Last I knew, Orinthian forces were gathered in Lou, and Auntican forces were near the border. Both sides hadn't attacked yet. Both were waiting to see who would make the first move."

Alida sighed in relief. She wondered where her father was and how he was doing. Hopefully, he was safe in Abdul but, knowing him, he would want to join the fight. Rider would have also gone to join, but she wasn't as worried about him.

"I'm glad to hear it."

"Me as well."

"So, you're a loyal Orinthian citizen?"

Cael looked taken aback. "Of course I am. Why do you ask?"

"You would be surprised to think about how many Orinthians don't give a shit about what happens to our country," Alida said, thinking especially of Roman and his profit-driven life.

"I do what I do because I love Orinth and I care about our people."

"How did you come about this line of work anyways?" Alida asked him.

"I don't want to use the term family business, but I suppose that's what you would call it. My father did it, as did his father. We've dedicated ourselves to finding the True King and killing him. But I know you don't want to hear about that part of it."

"I get it," Alida confessed. "I understand what you're doing and why. I don't have to agree with it, but I understand."

"That's good to hear, Princess- I mean Alida. You and I are more alike than you think. We do what it takes to protect Orinth. We just have different ways of going about it."

"You know who the True King is, you said?" Alida asked, ignoring the last part of his statement. They weren't alike. She did what she had to do as long as it didn't hurt anyone. But the more she thought about it, the more she realized; she would hurt someone if it meant protecting her people. She would make those sacrifices to keep them safe.

"Yes, we do. We've known for a long time. Our researchers have confirmed it time and time again. Our spies and our people know it to be true. We've lost him more than once. For the last twenty years, we've been trying to kill him, but it's hard to kill someone who's almost invincible. And this man, he knows how to use his power."

"If you don't mind my asking, who is it?" She hoped to the gods he didn't say Rider's name, although the gods had not been kind to her lately.

Cael narrowed his eyes at her. "You're not going to find out his identity and try to warn him, are you?"

She shook her head. "Maybe you're right and it's better if he's dead. I won't do anything to interfere. I just want to know," she lied.

"Fair enough. His name is Auden Frae."

Alida raised both eyebrows. "Auden Frae?" she repeated.

He nodded. "Yes, Auden Frae. He is a man from Orinth. We don't know exactly how he came to be the True King. But when he was fourteen years old, he killed a boy in an alley. Our people found the body and knew that it was the shadow. It didn't take long to find the identity of the killer. Since then, we've been trying to kill him, but he's good. He's been very alert and very aware. His powers are strong, and he's killed a lot of our men defending himself. We've been so close to killing Auden Frae, so many times. Almost my whole life has been spent in search of him."

Alida tried to talk but couldn't. Rider had been attacked in an alley when he was fourteen. Rider had the shadow. Rider was powerful. Rider was the True King. Yet, Cael claimed it was Auden Frae. Which meant Rider was Auden Frae. But how? He had promised he wouldn't lie to her again, so why hide the fact that he was named Auden Frae? What else had he not told her about his life before being the king's advisor? She was confused and distraught, on top of being in pain and exhausted. But she wouldn't give Rider away to Cael.

"Are you close to finding him?" Alida questioned him.

Cael sighed. "No. We're not, which scares me. At some point, Cassia will figure out that you don't have the blood of Arca. And then, she'll be on the search for him as well. If we can puzzle out his identity, she can as well. We have to get to him before she does."

"When did you find out about Cassia?"

"We have Auntican spies who spoke of the king's mysterious new lover. With a little research, we found her identity. How she got here and why she wants to open the wall, we don't know."

Alida explained to Cael what Cassia had informed her of her plan. He paled significantly.

"Well, shit," he said when she finished. "That isn't great."

"This war shouldn't be between Auntica and Orinth. It should be between everyone and Cassia."

"Will you tell your father?"

"If I find him, I will. But I don't know where he is, and I don't even know the first step to finding him. Even if I did, he's not stopping this war. The tension between our countries has boiled over. My father wants this war to happen because he's confident we can win it. But if Grafph was the one to stop the war, if he tried to talk with my father and tell him what was really going on, instead of me, well, maybe something would happen." Alida took a long, deep breath. The air was so fresh here, but it seemed to be choking her lungs tonight.

"Do you believe it could work?" Cael asked.

"I'm not sure. I thought from the beginning we should try to solve it with diplomats instead of fighting. But what do I know?"

"Probably a lot more than the people who always want to fight."

"My father and his advisor tricked me into leaving by making me think I was the Last Heir. I thought that I was protecting my people by going, by preventing Grafph, or Cassia, I suppose, from capturing me. Instead, they just wanted me to leave to be out of danger. They knew I wasn't the Last Heir. They thought it was safer for me elsewhere than in Orinth." Over the course of the last few weeks, she had realized this. Rider knew he was the True King, but allowed Alida to embrace the possibility it could be her in order to shelter her.

"Are you upset about it?" Cael asked.

Alida shook her head. "Maybe I was at first. Them tricking me to protect me? Then I realized that they were doing it because they loved me. And they were right. If I was knew that I wasn't the Last Heir, I wouldn't have gone anywhere. I would've stayed in Orinth and fought. I guess in the end, it didn't matter. Cassia still caught me, and if it wasn't for you and your men, she would've killed me."

"So, what's next for you then, Alida? Go back to the castle and recover? Or join the frontlines and fight Auntica?"

"Actually, I was going to see if I could join the Society of the True King."

She had thought about it over the last two days. After being taken by Cassia, she now had two goals. Her first one was to protect Rider. No matter what he had done or the lies he had told her, he was still her brother. She loved him and she always would. She would not let the Society of the True King kill him, even in the name of the safety of Orinth. The only way she could make sure that they never found the man was to be close to them, watch their every move, and warn Rider if they were getting too close. After talking to Cael, she liked what the Society stood for: protecting innocent life. Her whole life, she had felt useless. This was her first chance to actually work to help Orinth. The second goal was simple. She wanted to be the one to kill Cassia Messina. She wanted to take her knife and plunge it into her chest and watch the look in her eyes as she realized that Alida had won and Orinth had won. If she stayed with the Society of the True King, Alida would have a chance at being that person. And with the gods as her witness, she would be that person.

Cael looked shocked. "You what?"

Alida took a breath. "I know what you're thinking. I'm the Princess of Orinth and I would have nothing to contribute to the group."

"I wasn't thinking that at all," Cael replied. "You've just taken me by surprise is all."

"I want to fight against Cassia, not Auntica."

"I respect that."

"But?"

"Nothing. If you want to join us, then I'm not going to stop you."

Alida almost gaped. "You're serious?"

Cael smiled at her. "Of course I'm serious. If anyone has a justified vendetta against Cassia right now, it's you."

Alida clasped her hands together. "I was expecting a lot more fight than that."

"Well, you won't get any. You're right. We need to find Grafph and tell him the truth, even if we have to pound it through his brain. Your father is right to be defensive. If we told him he needed to stop the war, he wouldn't. But if

Grafph called off his forces? That would be another story. We could unite Auntica and Orinth again and focus on the real enemy: Cassia."

"My thoughts exactly."

"We'll have to run it past the Society's leader when we get back to Tilda and then we'll leave right away."

"Wait, aren't you the leader?" Alida asked.

Cael laughed. "Oh right. I ran it past me and me says yes."

Alida beamed. "Good, I'm glad. You already have an advantage. I'll be able to get an audience with Grafph with no problems."

"We'll talk about exact strategy at our base in Tilda. But that is a possibility."

Alida felt herself grow slightly happier at the development. There. She could protect Rider and take down Cassia all in one. She would be sabotaging them and helping them at the same time. Her mind froze up; was she smart enough to make this work? Then, she immediately rejected that idea. The last month of her life had been spent pretending to be Nova Grey and people had believed her, the princess of Orinth. She could pull off more deception and no one would question it.

"Thank you, Cael," Alida said, turning to look into his grey eyes. "Truly, I appreciate it. I wasn't sure where I was going to go and what I was going to do. I was afraid of being useless again but now, I know I can do some real good."

Cael stood up. "In my opinion, and I don't know how much my opinion means to you," he smiled again, "I don't think you've ever been useless. At least from what I've heard." He reached down towards her and Alida grabbed his hand. He pulled her to her feet and shot her the same smile.

Alida returned it. "I appreciate that."

"You should try to get some sleep. You look like you need it." He grinned and started walking back towards his camp.

Surprisingly enough, that night, Alida managed to close her eyes and drift into a fitful sleep.

Chapter 10

Tilda Orinth

"Where are we?" Alida asked him. The next morning, Cael had offered to let Alida ride with him, instead of bouncing around between men. She had accepted, gladly. Not that the men weren't kind and courteous, but she always felt like an imposition. She knew Cael a little better than the rest of them, so she didn't feel as bad.

They had awakened early in the morning and made the short ride to Tilda. They had been riding through the city streets for almost an hour. Alida wondered if they were going in circles. She could just see the harbor and smell the salt of the sea, and it made her sad. She had missed that smell, and as much as she hated to admit it, missed sailing. Tilda, however, was a beautiful city. Cobblestone streets with large, colorful buildings made it appealing to the eyes. It was one of the wealthier cities in Orinth, after Tenir and Abdul.

They ended up in the downtown area, full of only shops and restaurants. The city was split into three large sections: the downtown, the business sector, and the residential section, with the harbor falling just beyond the three. It was easy to navigate. Alida wished, suddenly, that they were here just for fun, instead of planning a war against a demon. She would've enjoyed walking the streets, stopping into shops, sipping wine on terraces of different restaurants. It reminded her of Rein and the time she had spent there before boarding The Valley, when there had been significantly less pressure on her than there was now.

They had stopped in front of a tavern that Alida didn't recognize. It was a few stories tall and made of an old brick that reminded her of Abdul. The architecture was so similar to home it made her heart ache to return.

"What are we doing?" Alida asked.

"We're getting breakfast, of course," Cael said, steering into one of the alleys, where there were hitching posts for horses. He jumped off the back and helped Alida down as the rest of the men began tying up their own mounts. That was another convenient thing about Tilda; it catered to horses because of the number of tourists who traveled through it.

"I don't have any money," Alida said, and Cael just rolled his eyes, smiling.

They walked into the door of one of the buildings on the street. As soon as they stepped in, Alida stopped.

Sahar and Roman were sitting at one of the tables, watching as they walked in.

"What is this, Cael?" Alida yelled, taking a step back. Her heart seized up with a mix of shock, fear, but more prevalent than anything, anger.

Cael held his hands up in surrender. "Just give them a chance. Alida, they were the ones who told me you had been taken."

Alida ignored her surprise at that statement and snapped at him, "They were the reason I was taken in the first place, Cael. I should be in Nagaye right now."

"Just hear them out, Alida. And if you don't like what they say, we can leave."

Alida turned around. "I'm leaving right now."

Sahar stood up and said, "Alida, wait. It's me you're mad at, not him."

Alida turned back around to face the captain. "You're exactly right, Sahar. I don't think I would use the word mad, however. Try incredibly pissed? Or maybe it's taking all of my willpower not to smash your faces in right now."

Cael started laughing.

"Give me a chance to explain," Sahar pleaded. "Please. And then you'll never have to see me again. Just give me that."

Maybe it was the way her voice cracked at the end, something Alida had never heard before. Sahar was many things, but vulnerable was never one of them. Except just now. Alida glanced at Cael, who nodded at her. She had only met the man days ago, but he and his men had saved her from Cassia and from certain death. She was willing to give him a chance, but only one.

"Fine," Alida said, stomping over to the table. Yanking the chair out, she sat in it, across from them, and crossed her arms. "You have five minutes. Or should I make it less? Is it possible to get Auntican guards here in five minutes to turn me in again?"

Roman snorted but said nothing. Alida shot him a look. He looked annoyingly as good as he always did, in a black shirt that made his arms look bigger than they really were. Sahar was dressed in her usual badass garb, paired with a bandana around her long hair.

Cael slipped into the chair next to her as she spoke first, "What is it?"

Roman and Sahar exchanged a glance, which immediately made Alida furious. They were always exchanging little glances, talking in their own language as if no one else existed. Sahar turned to Alida. "I guess we should start by telling you what happened after we turned you in," she said, all traces of vulnerability gone, replaced by the hardened captain.

Alida raised an eyebrow.

"They took you into that room. We asked what was going to happen to you and the guards just laughed in our faces. We were terrified because we didn't know who we had just given you to. They had already paid us but truly, we didn't want any harm to come to you. We thought it was a political game, but we quickly realized it was more than that."

"It took a little digging around, but Roman is good at that kind of stuff. We got in contact with Cael, actually. And that's when we found out about the Last Heir and the sacrifice at the Shadow Wall. We know, now, that was what you meant when you said you were going to die. And well, as much as you hate us, Alida, we never wanted you to die. You don't understand, we thought we were doing what was best for our business. But we were wrong. We were also wrong to believe this war didn't concern us. You're right; we're Orinthians first. Grafph is trying to destroy the Shadow Wall. That concerns everyone. I know this won't help, but I am truly sorry. I know you'll probably never be able to trust me again, but I am. I made a mistake. It's hard for me to admit that I'm ever wrong."

"I want to help Orinth. I've stopped operations with smuggling, until this is all over. We want in on the fight. So, we need to know what you think we should do. To kick Auntica's ass," Sahar finished.

Alida just stared. It was a lot to process and she wasn't sure she should trust her. But Cael did.

"You're the ones who sent Cael after me?" she asked.

Roman nodded. "We've known him and the Society for a long time. They use us for transport, and we use them for information. We knew he wouldn't be okay with an innocent woman dying in the name of the Shadow Wall."

Alida looked at her hands and took a deep breath. "I...thank you. They saved my life. I was close to dying and they saved me. I wouldn't have been there in the first place if it weren't for you, but that's beside the point. You swear you actually want to fight for Orinth? This isn't some kind of trick?"

Sahar shook her head. "Orinth has given me everything. It's given me my business, my ship, my livelihood. I owe it and if fighting to keep it safe is the price I have to pay, I'll pay it without a question."

"What about your husband?" Alida asked.

Sahar sighed. "Dax is gone," she said. "I know it now. I've been searching for a long time, but I think I've always known. He's gone. I can't keep holding out for him." Her fingers were drumming the table and Alida couldn't help but notice the slight tremble in them.

"Are you sure?" Alida asked her. She wasn't Sahar's biggest fan at the moment, but she had always felt sympathy about her situation with her husband. His name was Dax, the man the captain had fallen in love with and married soon after she left the brothel. He had disappeared on a journey to Nagaye. It was because of him that Sahar had started sailing in the first place, and yet, they had found no trace of him. Alida had prayed to the gods that Sahar would find the man she loved, but right now, it seemed she had given up.

Sahar nodded. "Yes, I am. I think Dax would rather I help my country than look for him. We've made enough money to stop our operation for a bit, at least until this is all over. It's our incentive. The faster we can defeat Auntica, the faster we can start back at it again."

"This isn't just some way to absolve your guilt about turning the Orinthian princess over to her death, is it?" Alida asked.

Cael snorted and Roman narrowed his eyes. "No, it's not that," he said. "I happened to like Nova Grey a lot better anyways."

Alida shrugged. "I did too."

He smiled at her, the first one she had seen from him in a while, since their day in Aram. "We're being serious, Alida. We want to help. I thought that it was all about profit, but it's not. Tell us what to do."

Alida glanced at Cael, who was watching her. "Guys, I'm not a general or a leader by any means. I don't know where you would be best suited. I almost want to tell you to go ask my father. He would know where you're best suited."

Sahar shook her head. "No, he wouldn't. All due respect to the man, but to him, this is just about the war. You know what the stakes are. You know about the Shadow Wall and the Last Heir. But most importantly, out of anyone in this room or this country, you have the most to lose if this goes wrong. That's normally the best motivation for anyone. You're smart and you're resourceful. We're going to listen to you."

Alida bit her lip. "I appreciate it," she said.

Roman leaned back and put his hands behind his head. "So what will it be, Miss Goulding? Do we gear up and go fight some Aunticans or go destroy Illias or what?"

She thought about it for a long time before answering. "I want you to go to the Northern Continent."

All three of them looked taken aback, Cael included. "What?" Sahar said.

"The Northern Continent has never declared allegiance to either Auntica or Orinth. They've never been a part of our wars, but this isn't just about our two countries anymore. If the wall comes down, we're all screwed. That's how you'll convince them. The Pareshin."

Sahar raised both eyebrows. "The Pareshin?"

"You've heard of them?"

"Of course, I have, in stories and songs sung in taverns. I didn't know they were real."

She hated to admit it, but Alida was only partly sure herself. She had heard rumors of the group of soldiers in the North, skilled warriors who trained from birth and were considered the most dangerous in the world. She was familiar with the stories of these men taking on twenty enemies alone and leaving unscathed. They were separate from the countries in the North but often worked for hire. There were whispers of them being otherworldly, possessing powers that humans didn't have. The Pareshin were deadly, and if she wanted anyone to take on Cassia Messina, it would be them and only them.

Alida had heard about magic her entire life. She had heard that the Forest Dembe was magic. She had heard that the people of the Darklands were skilled wizards. She wasn't sure what to believe, after coming to find out her best friend/brother had the power of the shadow. His power came from behind the wall, but she wasn't sure if other magic even existed. And if it did, from where did it originate? It was hard for her to believe the Pareshin had magic. But she knew that they had to be strong, and she wanted them on her side. Because, apparently, she was leading the strike against Cassia Messina.

An army of normal soldiers wouldn't suffice against a demon. The men who were with her, she quickly found out, were also influenced by her power somehow. They were faster and stronger than regular people, as if Cassia was pouring her own strength into them.

Taking them on with the Pareshin would be a different story, if the rumors were indeed true.

She explained her thinking to Sahar and Roman, who sat in stunned silence. She told them who Cassia was and her mission to destroy the wall. Finally, Alida described why the Pareshin would be the best to defeat the woman and her own army.

After a long period of silence, Sahar said, "It would make sense. If we're really going to try to kill this Cassia, we need the most powerful army we can find."

Cael chimed in. "Alida, my men didn't have any problem with her men. Are you sure you want to spend the time doing this?"

"Your men had no problem because they weren't attacking her men. You were only helping me escape. You set a diversion and then we all ran. If you had to go head-to-head with them, and no offense, I'm sure it would have been a slaughter."

Cael snorted. "I'm not sure I agree, but I think I see your point."

"Cassia Messina should've died once. She waited in the Shadow Realm for a thousand years. We can't guarantee that she would really die if we killed her again. She could find another way to come back," Alida said.

"So, what do we do?" Roman asked. "If we can't just kill her and she's impossible to fight, what is the plan here?"

Alida shook her head. "I don't know. I truly don't know. All of my being wants to kill Cassia and watch her burn, but she prevented herself from going to the Beyond once. She could do it again. There has to be some way to make sure she stays dead."

Cael spoke up, "I will have my researchers get right on it. Not that there's a lot to go on. There are few people alive know how to make someone stay dead."

"Well, it's a start," Alida said. "And while we're figuring out how to kill her, we have to make sure she stays away from the True King, whoever it is. I'm going with Cael to speak with Grafph. First, we need to see if Cassia has some sort of hold on him. If she does, well, we will go from there. Regardless, we need the war to stop between our countries and the war against Cassia to begin. And if you agree, Sahar and Roman, you can go convince the Pareshin to be our frontline."

Sahar and Roman exchanged glances once more. "We'll have to talk to the crew about it," Sahar finally replied. "Sailing to the North will be a long, tough journey. We'll have to travel through the Auntican Straight and up the Sea of

Theroe. And even then, I've never been to the North. I don't know where to find the Pareshin and how I would convince them. Maybe they could be bought."

"Everyone can be bought," Roman chimed in. "Take it from me, every person can be bought. I'm surprised my father doesn't already have connections with these Pareshin. I'll check with him before we go. If we go. Like Sahar said, we need to talk to the crew."

"Is that a no then?" Alida asked.

Sahar stared at her. "You know me, Nova. I'm never one to back down from a challenge."

Alida smiled wickedly at her. "Obviously not. But this is more than just a challenge, I believe."

Roman spoke, "We owe you one, Alida. We owe Orinth one. If this is what you think is the best thing for us to do, then we'll find a way to do it." Sahar nodded, agreeing with his statement.

"I know you will." Alida looked over at Cael, who had a slight smile on his face. "But are you sure you want to put your faith in me? Sahar, you've been captain of a ship for a long time and a successful entrepreneur. Roman, you're a Vacci for gods' sake, you know what you're doing. And Cael, you're the leader of the Society. You are all more experienced than I am at this. Believe me, I am open to any advice you can give me. All I've been doing is running charities and kissing babies since I was seven years old. I'm asking you again. Are you sure?"

None of them spoke until Cael opened his mouth. "Yes, Alida. It's as simple as that."

"And I'm not just a Vacci," Roman said, smiling. "Sahar is more than just the captain and Caellum is more than just the leader of the Society. I know you don't trust us yet, Alida, but together we can be a team. We can take down Cassia and Grafph and anyone who's threatening Orinth. We're like a brotherhood."

"Sisterhood," Sahar and Alida said at the same time and then exchanged a sly smile. Alida felt her heart lighten. Roman was right. It would take a while for her to trust the pair of them again, but she had missed them both. She had missed her friendship with Sahar and constantly teaming up on Roman Vacci.

Roman smirked. "Alright then. Sisterhood."

"And we're going to kill Cassia Messina for what she did to you," Sahar finished.

It was becoming hard not to immediately fall into the pattern of being her friend again.

Sahar and Roman decided to go talk to the crew immediately and return with an answer. If the crew declined to pursue and recruit the Pareshin, then they would figure out a new way to contribute. It lifted Alida's spirits immensely and she was happier than she had been in a while. The pain still lingered, but it was gradually numbing. She was alive and she was actively fighting against the person trying to destroy her world. Rider was alive somewhere. She was getting her friends back. It was coming together again.

Alida and Cael stayed in the tavern and ordered breakfast, not talking about the war anymore. They chatted for a little bit, but mostly ate in silence. She knew that there were so many thoughts running through both of their minds, about the decisions they had just made and the repercussions they could have. It was almost thrilling to have that responsibility again, but simultaneously terrifying.

They had almost gotten through the entire meal unscathed, when the ground shook.

At first, Alida thought it was in her head, but Cael's eyes widened.

"That wasn't just me?" Alida asked as their empty breakfast plates vibrated. She looked around the room. They were the only customers in the small place and the rest of the empty chairs rattled. The glasses set out on tables started falling and suddenly the roaring of it filled her ears. Glass breaking, chairs falling, a thunderous roar. She could barely stand because of the tremor and she had to use her hands to support herself. Cael shouted something to her, but she could no longer hear. Instead, he just grabbed her hand and pulled her out of the place.

It appeared others could feel it as well. Dozens of citizens were running out of their homes and businesses, looking around for a sign of where it was coming from. A natural tremor was almost unheard of in Orinth, but it was exactly what it felt like. The buildings shook as if they were in a great wind, yet they did not fall. Tilda was a strong city and was built to endure the storms of the Wilds that sometimes drifted to them.

"What's going on?" Alida shouted to Cael, who watched the sky with an intensity she hadn't seen before.

"This isn't normal," was all he replied. "Something's happening."

"What's happening?"

"Cassia."

She felt her heart drop. She hoped to not have to see the woman again until she was physically and mentally prepared to fight her and win. Instead, she was fraught with the mental and physical exhaustion of their encounter. She remembered, abruptly, how Rider was able to find her in the caves. All he needed was an object that belonged to someone, and he could track them down using the shadow.

Alida closed her eyes. "She's coming back for me," she whispered.

Cael looked at her. "How is she doing this? I know the shadow is strong but strong enough to shake the ground? It's unheard of."

"She's going to destroy the city."

"We have to go."

"No, Cael, I have to go to her."

Cael looked like she had slapped him in the face. "Um, no. I don't think so."

"She's going to destroy the city if I don't. This is her gambit: force me to turn myself in or destroy a city of my country."

"Alida, we just saved you from her and it wasn't easy. You can't offer yourself up to her. Do you remember the way she treated you?" he said, exasperated.

"Do you want Tilda to be destroyed by this?" she yelled at him.

He threw his hands into the air as another intense shake caused the buildings around them to falter. It was only a matter of time before the cracks would form and they would fall. They were built to face storms but not shadow-induced tremors.

Alida touched his arm and said, "Thank you for everything. I would've liked working with you," and then she began to run.

She heard him call after her, but she was already on the move, towards the outskirts of Tilda where she had awakened only hours ago. It was hard to run when the ground was constantly shifting and people were standing, waiting to see what was about to happen. They were terrified and it was because of her. She had to make Cassia stop this. She had just told a group of people that she would do anything to protect Orinth and that included dying for it. She thought she had escaped her and could spend her time fighting but maybe this was how it was supposed to be from the beginning.

Rider and her father had told her she was the Last Heir to protect her and send her out of the country, yet she never made it. She believed that she had to be killed to destroy the Shadow Wall, yet it turned out not to be true. But maybe, just maybe, she had been meant to die from the start. Maybe it had all been inevitable and even with all the work and sweat and tears, she still had to die.

Except she didn't see Cassia when she ran out of the city streets.

In the distance, in the field not far from where they had camped, she saw two figures standing across from one another. From here it was almost impossible to see their faces, but they stood about ten feet apart, a force radiating from them. The shadow was what was causing the tremor, but it wasn't from one or the other. They were fighting and the shaking of the world was a side effect of their immense power.

The wind blew Alida's hair like crazy as she started running towards them.

Because one of them had to be Rider.

Chapter 11

Orinth-Wilds Border

She was sitting with Adriel, overlooking the Wilds. This was his favorite place. She couldn't remember how she had ended up here with him, but she didn't care. He had his arm wrapped around her and she was snuggled into his shoulder and it fit so perfectly. His wool blanket covered them both, protecting from the chill, allowing them to simply sit back and enjoy the view.

And wow, the view. Mountains and trees and so much green. Sawny had never seen so much green before. The sun was just beginning to set, and the sky was pink, orange, and red. It was such a special scene, and she couldn't think of someone better to watch it with than Adriel.

"Adriel?" she said, looking up at him.

He looked down at her in a way no one had ever looked at her before. There was love and care and affection in his eyes as if she was the only other person in his world. She wished she could just stay in his sight forever. "Yes?" he asked, planting a small, soft kiss on her forehead.

"Do you think I'm a good person?" she asked him.

"No, Sawny. You're a murderer. You're a terrible person and you deserve to die," he responded, still smiling at her and suddenly she couldn't breathe. She tried to open her mouth to scream, but nothing came out. Adriel seemed frozen, smiling at her, but his eyes far away.

And then Auden was shaking her awake.

"Sawny, you were starting to scream," he said, his hands on her shoulders. "Are you alright?"

Sawny tried to shake herself out of it, but she could hear Adriel's voice echoing in her head, back and forth and back and forth. "I'm sorry, it was just a bad dream." She peered around his shoulder where she could see the smoke from a distant camp. They had finally come out of the thick forest of the Wilds and were in the fields between the Wilds and Tilda. "Do you think they heard?" she asked him.

Auden shook his head. "We're pretty far away from them," he said, releasing her and looking over his shoulder at the smoke.

The last few days they had tailed the woman and her group of black-cloaked soldiers. The group of people who had previously held Alida were now tracking her. The woman who had the power of the shadow and neither Auden nor Sawny could figure out how. But Alida was Auden's sister and Sawny's...aunt. She wasn't sure she could get used to it, but she knew she had to help save her. After all, Alida's blood wouldn't affect the wall at all. It would be Sawny's. She wouldn't let an innocent girl die in her place.

They were going to follow them until they eventually found Alida or knew with certainty she was safe. Auden, without using his powers, was a skilled tracker. Sawny didn't want to ask how he could possibly be so good at everything. But then again, Sawny was somewhat of a tracker herself, taught by Caleb.

She wished Adriel were with them. He was on her mind constantly; in her dreams, but worse, in her nightmares. It was always Adriel telling her he hated her or telling her she was a monster. Most of the time, she would wake up herself, but Auden had finally taken notice tonight.

She would never see Adriel again and it felt like her heart was shattered into a million pieces. It wasn't necessarily whole to begin with. It had gone from already broken to just more broken than before. But right now, at least she had some drive. Once they saved the princess, she wasn't sure what she would do.

"You can go back to sleep," Auden told her. "I'll wake you when they start moving again."

Sawny raised an eyebrow. "I can take over the watch if you want to sleep."

Auden gave a small, tired smile. "I can't sleep anyways."

"Why not?"

He shrugged. "It's been a very interesting couple of days."

"You can say that again," Sawny said with a quiet laugh.

"Every time I try to close my eyes, I think about her. And you. And the years that I've let go by me without knowing you existed. There was always this small part of me that thought I would see her again, when I had it all figured out.

But she's gone and I don't know why. Anyways, it's easier to keep myself occupied with other things."

Sawny felt a burst of raw emotion in her chest and took a deep breath to settle it. "I know what you mean," she said, trying for a smile, but it came out more as a grimace. "It's kind of what I've been feeling like for the last four years. Always wondering who killed her and my father."

"Caleb?"

"Yes. I'm sorry, is it weird if I call him father in front of you?"

Auden shook his head. "Not a bit. After all, he is more of your father than I'll ever be. He raised you, and from what I've heard from you and read in the letter, he was a good husband to Marvie. I owe him everything."

"He was a good father," Sawny took a breath. "I...but it doesn't mean..."

Auden held a hand up. "Sawny, you don't have to say anything to appease me, truly. He's your father, but you just happen to have my blood. We don't have to pretend it's something else."

Sawny was taken aback. "So, you don't want to be a part of my life?" she asked, slightly hurt.

"Of course I do. I just found out I have a daughter, whose mother I love more than life itself. Well...loved. I want to be a part of your life, but I don't want to force you to accept me."

"You don't have to force me to. We can work out the details later, but I'm not kicking you out of my life just yet."

Auden smiled. "I'm glad to hear that."

Sawny opened her mouth to reply when she heard Cassia and her men start to ride again. Auden looked up. Sure enough, the first light of the morning was beginning to take the sky.

"I guess they're getting an early start," he said, starting to pack their various items onto Indira, who was tied near their camp. "We should hurry," Sawny agreed and helped him to pack the remaining items, feeling slightly better after the nightmare because of her conversation with Auden—her father.

Auden led Indira this time with Sawny sitting behind him as they started towards the direction where the group had been. Auden was tracking based both on their tracks as well as his pull to the woman's power. It was a beacon for him, the old, evil, powerful magic that she somehow possessed. It made her hard to lose. They had been concerned, at first, of losing the woman and her group of men. It would be easy for twenty horses to pull ahead from their one, especially exhausted Indira. But they traveled slower than they could've, frequently stopping. For that reason, keeping up with them hadn't been an issue.

They rode in silence for most of the morning, occasionally partaking in small talk, but mostly absorbed in their own thoughts. Sawny was fine with it. She had a lot on her mind, and she knew that Auden did as well. It was probably better if they both took time to think.

Where was Adriel right now? Sawny wondered. He had ridden out of that cave with no supplies except the clothes on his back and the various weapons he always had on him. Gods, she hoped he was okay. But of course he would be okay. He was back in his home, the Wilds. He knew how to survive. Where would he go? According to him, going back to his village and his tribe was no longer an option, seeing he hadn't killed his brother's killer. Would he lie to them? Make them believe that he had fulfilled his oath, that he had avenged his brother and the six other men that her father had killed? And then what? Adriel would settle down. He would marry a girl from his tribe, with the permission from the elders. He would forget about Sawny and the time they had shared together, the danger and the adventure of it all.

Maybe it was better that way. Auden had left Marvie to keep her safe. Adriel leaving her and not being a part of her life would keep him safe. She couldn't even force herself to hate him.

If only she could go back to that moment in time at the inn and choose not to go after Alida. But she was her blood, one of two of her only relatives who were alive. Sawny had to save her.

But if she hadn't, Sawny and Adriel would've gotten to spend the night at the inn together. They would've awakened the next morning, whenever they wanted, not rushed. They would've eaten breakfast together and people probably would've mistaken them for a happy couple who had gone away for the weekend. They almost were. They would've enjoyed the leisurely ride to Abdul, where Sawny would have tracked down the "king's advisor" and then whatever happened next would be up in the air.

If it hadn't been her father who killed his brother, she would've let Adriel fulfill the oath. She had thought that the killer deserved to die. More so than that, she thought Adriel deserved to have his life back.

And then, Adriel would've come back to Illias with her. He had said as much, in one way or another. Maybe he would've gotten his own place or maybe, just maybe, he would've lived with her. Adriel would help her with cases, travel with her when they needed to. And when they weren't working, she would show him her city. She would take him up to the nice part of town and get her favorite foods from her favorite taverns. They would ride their horses over to the southern part of the River Iyria and he would teach her how to swim better, like they had in the spring in Orinth. They would ride down to the Forest Dembe but this time, for fun, because she was protected there now. They would get to know each other, not in a rushed, dangerous way, but in a way as if they were just two normal people. She longed for this, longed for him, longed for that future that might have been had she been a different person.

She would never get that future.

That future was as lost to her as her dead parents.

Maybe she was meant to be alone. It didn't matter now.

It was just another fork in the road of life that she had missed. Just as Auden had missed the fork in the road that led to getting to raise her, getting to be her father, getting to be Marvie's husband. Just as her parents had missed the fork in the road of fleeing this damned country and never having to worry about being threatened again. She had come to believe that life was a series of missed forks.

But it was that series of forks that we had taken or that we had missed that made us who we were. It was the series of missed opportunities that had led us to where we were. Maybe it was a good thing and maybe it was a bad thing, but Sawny was here, right now, because of the choices she had made. She was here because of choices others had made without her consent. As was Auden. As was every single person in the world. Did we even have control over our own lives or was someone, a higher power, making all the choices and we were under the illusion it was us? We were just treading water while the tide took us out and brought us in, and we thought we were swimming.

Auden and Sawny were at the bottom of a hill. Indira was starting to tire, Sawny could feel it. She prayed to the gods that they would find and protect the princess fast because her horse needed a few days off. A regular horse would probably be dead by now, but Indira was not a regular horse. As she climbed the hill, Sawny had a horrible feeling in her stomach that something bad was about to happen. It was the same feeling she had riding into the Forest Dembe. The same feeling when she had gone to save Adriel from the Orinthians, a sense that something terrible was about to occur.

They had been so cautious while following the woman and her men. Auden was a skilled tracker but also knew how far they needed to be away so they wouldn't be caught. He always remained close enough to the group to sense the woman's power and never let her out of his range. It had worked well so far. The more distance they covered, the closer they were to finding the princess, protecting her from the woman who had murdered a man in cold blood.

Once Auden and his sister were reunited, Sawny would be able to go back to Auntica. It was almost done, but the sense of despair lingered. It was just nerves, she told herself. She was so close. Home felt like it was within her reach.

As they reached the top of the hill, Auden froze. Sawny looked around his shoulder and stifled a scream.

There they were, the group that they had been tracking for two days. Except they had stopped and were turned around, looking directly at them on the horse. The woman on the white horse was leaning back nonchalantly, studying them with something of amusement on her face. The city of Tilda lay in the background, only a short ride away, but it was too late. They were in trouble. They were in very big trouble.

"I had a suspicion we were being followed," she said, her voice filled to the brim with laughter. "I wasn't sure. But here you are. Why don't you just tell us what you want, and we can all move on with our lives."

They were still about twenty feet from them. There would be time to turn around and gallop as fast as they could and hope that the woman didn't care enough to go after them. But Auden didn't move. Instead, he said, "Who are you?"

The woman raised an eyebrow and flipped her blonde hair. "Gods, it's been so long since I've been in this world that everyone has forgotten about me. It makes me a bit sad. But no matter. It won't be much longer until everyone will know."

"So why don't you give us a head start and tell us now," Auden said with traces of sarcasm in his voice.

Sawny bit back laughter. He was brave, she would give him that. Or stupid. One of the two.

The woman jumped off her horse. "My name is Cassia Messina. And who do I have the pleasure of meeting?"

She felt every muscle in Auden tighten. "You're lying," he said. "Cassia Messina has been dead for a thousand years." Apparently, he knew who she was, but Sawny didn't have the first clue. Cassia Messina?

The woman, Cassia, laughed gleefully. "Oh yes, she has. But it appears she's back, doesn't it?"

"What is this?" Auden said, his voice dark. Sawny could feel his power starting to bubble to the surface.

And apparently, Cassia could as well. She smiled, dangerously. "Well, isn't this a wonderful little turn of events. I can feel the shadow within you. I can feel it starting to get angry at me. And you know, the only people who have the shadow are very important to me. Now I'm going to ask you again and if you don't answer me, I'll kill your friend." Sawny froze. "Who are you?"

"My name is Rider Grey," Auden said. "And I wouldn't do that, if I were you."

Her eyes lit up. "Your power, Rider Grey, is strong. I think that means you might be the True King. Because the only person with power like that would be the True King. Am I correct?"

Auden said nothing, but Sawny could feel his power swirling around, biding its time. This was not going well. They needed to get out of here. She glanced over her shoulder. There were no men behind them. If Auden just turned the horse around and shielded them with his power, they could escape from this woman. Go for the forest just beyond the fields and hope for the best. Cassia believed at that very moment Auden was the True King. They were both in great danger. They had to run.

"I thought it was the princess," Cassia said. "I really did. And then, it turned out she was a giant thorn in my side. She ran away and delayed us catching her. Then, she was constantly trying to escape. I even heard she jumped off a ship. We eventually caught her, and she still tried to escape, even after we tortured her." Sawny stifled a gasp.

"Oh yes, she was a fighter. And then, as if things couldn't have gotten any worse, The Society of the True King came to save her. Funny, isn't it? The Society of the True King, who have been trying to kill you for so long, who have killed anyone close to you. But because the princess wasn't the True King, they decided they must save her from me."

Sawny couldn't breathe.

"But now, I just want to kill her. I'm still looking for the True King, but I've been biding my time for a thousand years now, you know. A little side journey going to murder someone I hate is fun, right? But now that doesn't seem so important because you're in front of me."

Auden took a breath. "You're right, Cassia Messina. I have no idea why you want to destroy the wall and I don't care. But here I am, the True King."

No. What was he saying? He wasn't the True King, and he knew it. He was trying to protect Sawny and Alida.

Cassia smiled gleefully. "Right. So, the way I see it, we can do this the easy way or the hard way. The easy way, I'll let your friend right there go," she said, looking at Sawny. "She's young and has a lot of life to live. You wouldn't want to ruin that, would you? I've heard a lot about you. You've killed before, but it was always to protect someone else, or yourself. The offer I'm giving you, you wouldn't have to kill anyone at all. Just give yourself up and then the girl goes free."

"Dad," Sawny whispered furiously in his ear. "You're lying to her and it's going to get you killed."

"Just trust me. And did you just call me Dad?" he whispered back, a small smile creeping back on his face. He dismounted the horse quickly, glancing up at Sawny.

Despite the situation, despite the odds that they were probably both going to end up dead, Sawny smiled. "I guess I did," she said down to him and then Auden's power exploded.

Sawny flew off the horse because of it and landed on her back with a loud grunt. Indira had been thrown back as well, but was on her feet, starting to panic. Sawny had to get over there to calm her, but she couldn't move. The amount of power in the air was immense and it wasn't just Auden's.

She looked up and saw Cassia had her hands thrown forward and was using her own power to defend from Auden's. Auden stood on his feet, his hands by his side, the wind blowing around him, making his curls fly around his face. His back was to her and his focus was on Cassia. Cassia's men had fallen off their horses and were trying to round them up, as they had taken off running as Indira was about to. The ground started shaking and that's when Sawny started to panic.

The air crackled and hissed with electricity. What were they trying to do? Sawny didn't want to dip into her power to find out because Cassia would sense it, sense that she had the power and realize she was the True King. But she needed to protect Auden. It was easy to tell that Cassia's power was different from his or hers. It was still originating from behind the wall, but it wasn't the same. Auden took a step back. He was beginning to falter. Sawny had to move. She glanced at Indira, who was in the same place. The world shook some more and Sawny tried to yell at the horse. She met her eye and tried to will her to stay in place. Her shadow reached out to the animal without her control and Indira was motionless. Sawny cursed, but Cassia was too preoccupied to notice the tiny release of power. Indira was safe. Now she had to help Auden.

She managed to stand on her feet, but the ground was shaking. Sawny screamed as suddenly a crack of lightning came out of the sky and towards

Auden. She didn't even blink as her power suddenly wrapped around him like a shield. She flew off her feet for a second time as the lightning hit her shield with such tremendous force. It was nothing like she had ever experienced before as the pain crackled under her skin and she tried to scream again, but she couldn't. It was choking her, blocking off her air passage.

Then she heard it. A scream that echoed through the field, through the power, through everything.

"RIDER!!!"

They both stopped. Auden collapsed to his knees and Cassia turned around, towards the source of the scream. Sawny jumped to her feet and ran towards him, kneeling beside him, ignoring the pain surging through her body. Auden was breathing heavily and sweat dripped off his skin. His eyes were rolled in the back of his head, and he was struggling to remain conscious. Sawny shook him back and forth. "Auden? Auden! Dad! You have to wake up!"

His pupils returned and he managed to mutter, "Who just yelled that?"

Sawny looked up. There was a figure in the distance running towards them. The soldiers' horses were in a chaotic mess, and they were trying desperately to calm them, but Cassia paid no mind. Instead, she had her eyes narrowed at the figure. Sawny tried to see who it was.

It was a woman, by the looks of it, hair flying behind her as she stumbled forward, through the fields outside of Tilda. Cassia suddenly smiled.

"Oh, how convenient! The Princess of Orinth herself." She turned back to where Sawny knelt by Auden, who was trying fruitlessly to get up. "Now that I know you're the True King, I'll have no problem killing her myself, this very moment." She turned to where the princess was running, almost a hundred feet from them.

Alida was running into a death trap.

Everything seemed to go into slow motion as Sawny stood up. She could clearly see Alida Goulding, the Princess of Orinth, a short distance separating her from the woman who wanted to destroy the world, who wanted to kill Alida at that very moment. Cassia threw her hands back and Sawny released the wave of power she had been saving up, from the anger at Adriel for leaving her after he had promised he wouldn't, the anger at Auden for leaving her mother, the anger that she had been hoarding forever. There was so much anger, an entire sea of it, that she had been carrying on her shoulders for so long, so very long. It was more deadly than it had been when it had awakened outside of Tenir, and it arose in her, a mass of power beyond her imagination.

She released it all to protect Alida. She released it all to destroy Cassia. Sawny cast her hands toward the woman.

She hit the wall of old, ancient power but penetrated through it. Her shadow was stronger, angrier, more forceful, more everything. Cassia screamed as she was thrown backwards. She landed on the ground several feet away, on her back, groaning. She wasn't moving, but neither was Auden. Alida had stopped, briefly affected by the surge of power. Sawny herself wasn't sure how she had done it. But in another way, she was positive she had known how she had done it.

Cassia, whoever she was, had the shadow and in a powerful way, but Sawny was the True King. There was not a person who walked the world who had stronger powers than she. For a brief moment, Sawny stared at where the woman laid and was overcome with a sense of pride, but not good pride. It was a dark, malicious pride, and something about it was addicting.

The moment passed and Sawny snapped back into reality.

Alida started running again, towards where Sawny had knelt by Auden. Cassia hadn't moved and Sawny kept a watchful eye. The men had stopped to stare at their fallen leader, but none dared to approach her. The shaking of the ground, the clashing of the power, had stopped. The wind had died and there was silence as Alida fell down next to Auden.

"Is he dead?" she cried, looking at Sawny. She realized that the princess had no idea who she was but was more concerned about Auden at the moment. How confused she must have been.

"No, he's just unconscious," Sawny said, feeling his pulse. His eyes were closed, and his breathing was strained, but it was there. Auden's power was strong and more experienced than Sawny's, but it was no match for Cassia, who somehow had gained the shadow. But Sawny remembered reading a certain passage when she was at Jare's. Regardless of who had the shadow, how long they had it, how skilled they were with it, the True King was the most powerful.

Sawny was the True King. She was the most powerful person in their world because she was the True King.

She tried to focus, but that fact was ringing loud in her mind.

Auden's eyes opened. He looked up at the both of them and something of a dazed, yet confused smile spread over his face. "Well, fancy seeing the both of you here."

"Rider, are you okay?" Alida said, looking worriedly at Sawny and then back down at him.

"There's no time," he said. "Cassia is going to wake soon. Sawny, you need to take Alida and go quickly. She knows now. She knows you're the True King and she's going to want to take you. Get as far away as you can. Hide. Run. But keep Alida safe."

Sawny shook her head. "I'm not leaving without you," she said firmly.

"The three of us can't fit on the horse. Plus, I can't move. Trying to stop her power, it took too much out of me. The two of you can't save me and escape yourselves. Sawny, you must go. If she gets you it's all over."

Sawny realized how blatantly drained she was as her eyes started to droop. The strike had depleted her shadow, briefly, but completely. She could already feel it starting to regain its strength, but she didn't know how long it would take and she knew for a fact there wouldn't be enough to stop Cassia for a second time. With a dread in her heart, she knew Auden was right.

"Rider, we can't leave you here," Alida sobbed, a tear slipping out of her eyes as she grasped his hand. "I just got you back. And you're my brother."

Auden smiled at her. "I knew you would figure it out yourself. I'm sorry, Lida. I am. There's so much I need to tell you, but you have to go. You have to save yourselves because you're the most important people in the world right now. I love you. I love you both but please, leave."

Alida shook her head. "No, Rider. We can't-"

Sawny saw Cassia stir and she interrupted the princess, "He's right. We have to go."

"But she'll take you. She might kill you," Alida choked.

Auden stared up at her. "Then I'll die getting to see my favorite person in the entire world one last time. But I don't think she'll kill me. She knows now it's Sawny she needs. She'll use me as bait, but Sawny must stay safe." He squeezed Alida's hand and then looked to Sawny. "I'm glad I got to meet you, if only for a couple days." Sawny couldn't find her voice to respond.

Auden turned back to Alida, "I love you. I'll always be with you. Now go!"

Alida wouldn't stand up, so Sawny grabbed her hand and yanked her away from Auden, who had slid back into unconsciousness. Cassia was sitting up as Sawny jumped onto Indira and pulled Alida after her, who was trying to move now, but kept looking back at Auden. She was crying, but it was hard for Sawny to hear with the ringing in her ears. Cassia, the woman who apparently was trying to destroy the Shadow Wall, knew that it was her she needed. That was what they had wanted to prevent at all costs, but now she would know. It was Sawny. She had just gotten her father back in her life and he had asked her to leave him. How was she doing it? How could she leave this man behind, Alida's brother?

More importantly, Sawny's father.

She kicked Indira in the side, and they took off, neither towards the Wilds nor Tilda itself, but south. Alida was sobbing now, screaming not Auden's name, but his other name, Rider. There was so much going on, so much running through her mind. The ringing in her ears hadn't ceased and her body still coursed with the shadow, but Sawny kept asking herself: was she doing the right thing?

She had to get herself and Alida to safety and then she could think about it.

Sawny gave what was left of the shadow to Indira for energy as they rode as fast as they could away from Cassia.

And away from the father whom she had just met, the father she now had to leave behind.

Chapter 12

On the Coast of Lake Orinth

Alida Goulding hadn't said a word to her.

To be fair, the princess seemed to be in a numb, shocked sort of state and Sawny didn't imagine she would be interested in talking to anyone. They had rode through the day, stopping finally at nightfall because Sawny thought she might pass out. She had never felt this drained in her entire life. She remembered Auden briefly mentioning when he used the shadow too much, it fed off his body's energy. That had to have happened to her because the moment she stopped the horse, she almost fell asleep right there.

But no, she couldn't. They hadn't eaten all day. It was cold. They needed to set up a small camp and then get moving again. They couldn't even take the time to build a fire because Cassia would eventually see where they had been. If she had been in the right state of mind, she would've suggested getting another horse for the princess, but her mind was whirling with so many emotions, she couldn't bring herself to suggest it.

Sawny passed Alida a bed roll and a package of jerky, which she took without comment. She noticed the princess opened her mouth as if to say thank you, but no sound came out. Instead, she turned around and went a few strides away to set up her bedroll. Sawny watched her briefly before setting up her own and managing to swallow down a couple pieces of jerky. They didn't taste as good as they had two months ago. Two months ago. She had left Illias two months ago. It was almost absurd.

And now? Where was she going to go?

Cassia knew she was the True King and could probably figure out, using that information, that Auden was her father. No, she didn't know her name or who she was, but from the old, ancient power she had fought only hours ago,

Sawny knew this woman wasn't to be underestimated. If she wanted to find Sawny, she would find a way to do it.

Sawny had gone from a quiet life as an investigator to being on the run from a woman who almost killed the father she had just met.

"I'm sorry," Alida suddenly spoke. She was sitting on her bedroll, staring at Sawny in a dazed sort of way. "You must think I have terrible manners. My name is Alida and thank you for saving my life."

"I know who you are and you're welcome. I suppose I should explain who I am, though." Sawny regretted how bitter she sounded.

Alida didn't seem to notice. "I'm a bit curious."

She took a deep breath. "My name is Sawny Lois. I am Auden...Rider's daughter."

Alida's mouth opened and then closed. "His...his daughter?"

Sawny nodded. "I only found out about it a little while ago," she said and then began to explain to the princess of her enemy country who she really was.

When she finished, Alida didn't speak. She could see her processing it and Sawny suddenly felt bad for the girl. Cassia had bragged about her poor treatment of the princess, specifically mentioning torturing her. Now, Alida was finding out that her older brother had a life he had never told her about.

"So, it's you," Alida finally said. "You're the True King?"

Sawny nodded. "I am."

"I'm sorry."

Sawny almost laughed. "Me too. But it was my power that kept Cassia from killing you because I'm the True King. So, I guess I'm not sorry."

Alida gave a small smile. "It's been an interesting couple of months."

Sawny couldn't have agreed more.

For the next hour, they traded their stories about what had happened over the last two months. Sawny listened as Alida told her about the old man in the woods, dancing in Rein, boarding a ship with two people and feeling like she finally had friends, only to find out they had betrayed her to the king of Auntica, betrayed her to Cassia. Alida explained who Cassia was and what she wanted, and went on to recount her experiences with her, the times where she had unleashed the shadow on the princess. Sawny had wondered what it was like to be on the receiving end of her power and the princess had described it. Thank the gods Alida had lived to tell. She spoke about the Society of the True King saving her life and taking her back to Tilda, ending finally with how the world started shaking and she ran, thinking she was giving herself up to save her people.

Sawny decided she liked the Princess of Orinth. Her half-aunt or whatever. She was strong and she was brave, and Sawny realized quickly that she cared about her country more than most royals did.

Sawny, in exchange, told her about her business in Illias and how she was hired by a man from the Wilds to find who had killed his brother in the caves to save the princess of Orinth. At this point in the story, Alida's mouth fell open as she realized the connection and Sawny just smiled and continued, speaking of her travels into the Forest Dembe, meeting the forest witch and giving her most painful memory to her. She left out the parts about falling for Adriel, but she suspected the princess was figuring it out. Sawny described their run-in with the Orinthian soldiers and her revelations in Tenir about the True King and who her real father is. Then, awakening her power because Adriel was kidnapped by a group of Orinthians who were going to kill him.

"I'm sorry for the way he was treated," Alida said at this point. "I'm ashamed my fellow countrymen would act that way towards you or him."

Then, Sawny explained how she heard about the Princess of Orinth being taken by her king and felt the need to come save her, a gut instinct.

Alida raised an eyebrow. "You came to the Wilds to rescue me?"

Sawny nodded. "Something told me I had to. We traveled up to the Wilds and had to stop because of a storm. There was a man and when he saw me, he screamed my mother's name. We came to figure out that he was my father. That he was also the one that killed Adriel's brother all those years ago. Adriel..." she sighed and glanced at the princess, who had her eyes narrowed, "Adriel left when I wouldn't let him kill my father. He didn't fulfill his oath."

Alida shook her head. "It's absurd he thought you were going to let him."

Sawny shrugged. "It's...complicated. Very much so. Anyway, afterwards, Rider and I continued the quest to find you."

"I guess I have good friends," Alida had laughed. "Or family members, I suppose."

Then finally, ending up in the field outside of Tilda, face to face against an ancient, powerful demon-woman. And now, here they were.

When Sawny had finished, they sat in silence for a long time, both seemingly processing it once more. So much had happened in such a short amount of time, it was almost unfathomable. Sawny was half-expecting to wake up in her apartment and find that none of it had actually happened. She knew she wouldn't be that lucky.

After a few minutes, Alida broke the silence with a sigh. "So, what now?" she asked her.

Sawny had no idea where to even begin. Her plan was to go back to Illias and resume her old life, but she knew now that was a silly dream. She had said she wanted no part in this war, but it was too late. She was basically the cause for the entire war. There was no possible set of circumstances in which she didn't get to be a part of this. Now, Auden was probably Cassia's captive. She would use him to find Sawny or to bait Sawny. Eventually, Cassia would probably kill him. She had no use for him, as he wasn't the True King. Sawny couldn't let that happen.

Auden was her father, and she realized she wanted a relationship with him. She wanted her father in her life. She had only known him for a few days, but she knew why her mother had fallen in love with him. He was a good man who cared a lot about the people he loved. And Sawny figured she was one of those people now. She wasn't going to lose him after just finding him.

Cassia was undeniably powerful. According to Alida, she had spent a thousand years in the Shadow Realm and had somehow absorbed the shadow from being there. She could wield it now. The only thing stronger than the power she had was Sawny's power.

But the problem was Sawny didn't know how to control her power, besides in large, wild strikes. Auden had spent many years learning to use his shadow, but she didn't have that time. She needed to be taught how to use it, because if they had any chance against Cassia, she would have to know everything there was to know about her shadow. She couldn't just rely on untamed emotion and anger to defeat the demon-woman.

Sawny had to find someone who could show her how to use this power. She didn't know who that person was, but she knew where to start.

Sawny took a deep breath and said, "I need to learn how to use my power. If we want any chance of killing Cassia, someone must have powers to match hers. No, not match. Powers to best hers."

Alida agreed. "She's strong."

"I'm going back to the Forest Dembe. Matahali will know what to do. She's the only other being I've met who has magic. I'll figure it out from there. And then, I'm going to go find my father," Sawny said.

Alida nodded. "That makes sense."

"What about you?" Sawny asked.

"I can't stay with you. Cassia was using her power to track me, and she knows we left together. I'll put you in danger. We just have to make sure, no matter what, she doesn't find you."

"As much as I would like to have a companion to travel with, you're right," Sawny admitted. She felt slightly disappointed. After traveling with men for two months, it would've been nice to spend time with Alida. She wanted to get to know the only other relative she had besides her father. The princess wasn't what Sawny had been expecting.

"Before I saw you and Auden, I was planning on working with the Society of the True King. We were going to go talk to Grafph."

Sawny was taken aback. "What? Why?"

"He thinks Cassia is his innocent lover and nothing more. We're going to try and convince him that she's trying to destroy our world. I know it's a long shot, but if we somehow do, we'll get both sides to stop fighting against each other, and start fighting against Cassia."

Sawny raised an eyebrow. "That will be a long shot."

Alida frowned. "Yes, it will. But there's no sense in not trying."

"Are you sure about that?"

She nodded firmly. "I've spent my entire life training in diplomatic relations. I think if anyone can get through to Grafph, it will be me. I'm not entirely sure on the details yet, but I'll figure them out. Don't worry about me."

"And if Grafph says no, kidnaps you, and holds you hostage?"

"I had a thousand-year-old demon hold me hostage and I'm still here. I don't think I have to worry."

Sawny grinned. "True." Her smile faded as she spoke again, "You said the Society of the True King?"

Alida nodded. "They were the ones to save me from Cassia."

Sawny took a breath. "Alida, I know we just met and everything, but I need to ask a favor from you."

Alida looked slightly taken aback. "You just saved me, Sawny. If it weren't for you, I probably would be dead by Cassia's hand. I couldn't have gotten away from there by myself. So yes, of course I can do something for you."

Sawny smiled a little. "It really wasn't that big of a deal." Her face went straight again. "The thing is, Cassia said something to Auden, before all of it started. Cassia said that the Society of the True King had been trying to kill him for his whole life. I didn't understand what she was talking about."

Alida paled and nodded. "It's true. I thought the Society was just a bunch of fanatics, but they want to kill the True King to protect themselves. They've never been able to. Rider has managed to stay hidden all this time. I think when he switched his identity, it threw them off and has ever since. But, regardless, I think it's ridiculous."

"My friend Jare told me they were spiritual and worshiped the True King. But they don't. You're right, it is ridiculous. But the thing is, Cassia also said the Society of the True King has killed people who are close to him."

Alida looked confused. "She did?"

Sawny nodded. "And the thing is, my parents..." her voice cracked a little, "I still don't know who killed them. But my mother and Auden were in love. I think it might have been the Society of the True King who killed my mother and adopted father. I don't know why. But I need you to try and confirm it with them."

Alida opened her mouth to speak, but Sawny held up a hand. "Wait, Alida. I'm not upset you're working with the Society. It seems to me they're working towards something good. It seems like their focus is defeating Cassia at the moment, and not finding me and killing me. They might know that Auden isn't the True King. I think you should go ahead with them to Illias and convince Grafph the truth about Cassia."

"But you want me to also figure out if they were the ones responsible for the death of your parents?" Alida asked.

"Yes, I do."

"And if they are the ones responsible?"

Sawny took a breath. "I don't know, but I'll figure it out."

"Then I can do that for you, Sawny."

She sighed in relief. "Thank you," she said. "Truly, thank you."

Alida shook her head. "I owe it to you."

"So how are you going to find the Society again?" Sawny asked her.

"They're still in Tilda. And Cael won't leave without me. They want to know I'm safe. They're probably looking for me right now. I'm the key to getting an audience with Grafph. I'll go back by a different route to avoid Cassia." Alida shivered. "I underestimated how much she hates me."

Sawny laughed. "She does indeed, but I think it's a good thing. You must have annoyed the shit out of her when she captured you."

Alida grinned wickedly. "Well, I don't think I was going to get off on good behavior anytime soon."

Sawny suddenly frowned. "What do you think happened to Auden?"

Alida bit her lip. "I don't know. I hope he's safe. He was in bad shape when we left him, but we had to. If Cassia would've gotten you, it would've been over. Rider will find a way to escape."

"As soon as I have a better grasp on my powers, I'll find him. Cassia won't kill him until she has me."

"She won't. He's the only way she'll be able to find you and he will never give you up."

Sawny agreed. "So we have some time. We need to be fast though."

"Yes, we will."

Sawny glanced at Indira. "I'll need her to get to the Forest Dembe. It's a long way away. We can stop in the next village and get you a horse."

Alida suddenly stood up, eyes wide. "There's no need," she said, in a faraway voice.

Sawny turned around. Behind them, there was a horse, with a saddle on it, with supplies. It was nibbling on grass a few yards from them, barely noticing they were even there.

"Starlight," Alida whispered.

"Who?" Sawny asked, eyes not leaving the horse.

The princess walked towards it. "It's Rider's horse. My father and I gave it to him for his birthday."

"He had said his horse had run away," Sawny said, watching Alida approach the horse, who immediately nuzzled into her hair. "I guess it found you."

She petted its neck. "He lost a bet to me," she whispered, "and I got to name him. So, I gave him the most girly name possible. Starlight. And now he's here."

Sawny smiled. "You don't need a horse anymore then."

Alida shook her head. "I don't understand how this is possible."

Sawny looked into the sky. "Maybe the gods haven't abandoned us after all."

Alida led Starlight over to the same tree Indira was tied to and secured his reins. "Maybe not," she laughed. "I thought they had, but maybe not."

The next morning, at first light, they packed up the small camp they had made. Sawny felt slightly better, but desperately tired. The shadow was replenished completely. She took a deep breath. It wouldn't master her. She was going to learn how to use it, how to control it, and then she was going to fight with it.

For the first time since her parents were killed, she had purpose. She knew she was supposed to be here for a reason. It wasn't a mistake that she wasn't murdered alongside them. Sawny had the power to rid the world of a great evil. It would be a long, uphill battle, and the chances of her dying were exceptionally high, but damned if she didn't try.

Matahali had told her. And later, her mother's last words in the letter had told her.

You are steadfast.

"Thank you again, Sawny," Alida interrupted her thinking as the princess climbed onto Auden's horse. Sawny had given her half of her supplies as well as one of her knives. Sawny herself had her bow and arrows strapped to her back once again and it made her feel complete, even if she didn't need it anymore. She had spent years of her life learning the skill and she wasn't done with it yet.

"You're welcome," Sawny replied. "I'm sad we didn't have more time to get to know each other. You are my Aunt Alida after all."

Alida snorted but smiled. Sawny returned it.

"I have no doubt I'll see you again," Alida said.

"Oh, you will. And then we can have a proper life catch-up, over a glass of Orinthian wine. Right after we kill Cassia Messina."

Alida suddenly jumped off her horse and approached where Sawny was standing next to Indira. She hesitated before wrapping her in a tight embrace.

Sawny was surprised, but she hugged the girl back. She was several inches shorter than her, but it felt so right to be hugging the princess. Her family.

They let go.

"Good luck," Alida said, climbing back onto Starlight.

"You, too," Sawny replied, mounting Indira. She had used her replenished shadow to give Indira more energy. She would ride a few hours and then stop to let her horse have a proper rest, when she was sure Cassia couldn't track the two of them.

"You know, when I was on the ship and pretending to be Nova Grey, part of my cover story was that I had four older brothers. I always bragged to Sahar about how cool my nieces and nephews were. I didn't know it was actually true."

Sawny broke into laughter. "Well, you're welcome. Not that there's much to brag about."

Alida raised an eyebrow. "Sawny, you literally knocked out a thousand-year-old demon-woman. I think you need to cut yourself some slack." She turned Starlight around, and said, "Until next time?"

Sawny smiled. "Until next time," she replied and Alida kicked her horse and was off.

Sawny watched her go until she was just a speck in the distance, traveling towards Tilda. She took a deep breath and thought about all that happened in the last two months, everything that had gone down and what it meant. But she was alive. And she had a job to do.

Sawny nudged Indira's side and she began galloping in the opposite direction that Alida had gone.

"Well," Sawny said to her horse. "Here we go again."

Acknowledgments

I would like to start by thanking my family for their constant support. I love knowing I can pursue my dream with your blessing. I would like to thank my dad for believing in this book and believing in me. Thank you to LeMay and Rem, the first to explore the world I created. Thank you to Savannah and Mom for everything you do for me, it does not go unnoticed.

Once again, thank you to the amazing group of editors who worked on my book. I can't get anything past you guys! Thank you to Grandma Sullivan, Kathy Lockwood, Lorelei Bond, Marilyn Harbin, Lisa Leach, and John Sullivan. Thank you again to Rose Cruz for providing so much inspiration from your incredible artwork.

Thank you to the friends who have my back and encourage and inspire me every day. You know who you are, and I promise, one day, I'll write characters in my stories after you.

Finally, thank you, reader, for joining the world of Fall to Darkness. This is a journey you aren't going to want to miss, so I'm glad you're along for the ride with me. If you enjoyed 'The True King', please consider leaving a positive review on Amazon, Goodreads, etc., or tell me all about it at: falltodarknessseries@gmail.com

Remember to check out our website, falltodarkness.com, for updates on upcoming books, release dates, merchandise, and more!

The Gatekeeper

Book #3 of the Fall to Darkness Series

Coming 2023…

'Marvolene'
A prequel to the events of 'The True King'
Available on falltodarkness.com

Glossary

- Abdul- the capital of Orinth and the home of the Orinthian royal family
- Adriel- the warrior from the Wilds who took an oath to see his brother's killer dead and hired Sawny Lois to help him find the killer
- Alida Goulding- the princess of Orinth, fled the country on The Valley to escape Auntican threats
- Arca- the first queen of Orinth and the first to possess the shadow; daughter of Cassia Messina and the demon Abdiah
- Auden Frae- Sawny's birthfather, as revealed by the letter her mother left for her
- Auntica- the country ruled by King Grafph and at war with Orinth; home to the Forest Dembe
- Cassia Messina- the lover of the demon who closed the wall, Abdiah, and mother to the first person to the possess the shadow, Arca
- Caleb Ore- Sawny's adopted father who was from the Darklands and killed by a group of mysterious people
- (the) Darklands- the country of warring tribes, with no connections to Auntica or Orinth
- (the) Dela- a river running through Orinth that leads to the Sea of Nagaye
- (the) Forest Dembe- the forest in the south of Auntica, the subject of much legend and myth, home to the forest witch Matahali
- Grady- a country across the sea from Orinth and Auntica
- Grafph- the king of Auntica, the main cause of the war with Orinth, actively seeking to destroy the Shadow Wall
- Ice box- an insulated cabinet or chest with a compartment for ice, used for preserving or cooling food, beverages, etc.
- Illias- the capital of Auntica and home to the Auntican royal family
- Jare Micheals- the keeper of records in Tenir and large player in the Orinthian black market
- (the) Last Heir- the last descendent of Abdiah with the blood to destroy the wall, given they are of the Orinthian royal line
- Ledger- the old man from the North living in the forest south of Abdul, Orinth

- Marvolene (Marvie) Pere/Ali Lois- the mother of Sawny, from Auntica but grew up in Tenir before fleeing back to Auntica, wife of Caleb Ore
- Matahali- the forest witch of Dembe and friend of Sawny Lois
- Nagaye- the desert country East of Orinth, across the sea of Nagaye
- Natasha Lyn- the former, deceased queen of Orinth, mother to Alida, wife to Tieran
- (the) Northern Continent- the continent to the north of Auntica and Orinth, home to the legendary warriors, the Pareshin
- Orinth- the country ruled by King Tieran
- Rider Grey- the advisor to King Tieran, best friend of Alida, and known wielder of the shadow
- Roman Vacci- the second mate of Sahar Bow, the youngest son of Damon Vacci
- Sahar Bow- the captain of The Valley, former prostitute, notorious smuggler of Orinthian wine
- Sawny Lois- an investigator from Auntica hired to find the killer of Adriel's brother, possesses the shadow
- Shadow- a power that comes from the other side of the Shadow Wall, capabilities such as bodily torture, manipulation, killing, locating others, and more
- Shadow Wall- the border between the human realm and the realm of darkness, not much is known about what dwells on the other side of it
- Tilda- the northernmost city of Orinth, closest to the Wilds and on the coast
- Tenir- the largest city in the south of Orinth, harbor city with prosperous sailing trade, and home to prominent Orinthian smugglers, headquarters of the Vacci family
- Tieran- the king of Orinth, father of Alida Goulding, leading the war against Auntica
- (the) True King- a theory that there is another person who actually has the blood of Abdiah, a bastard child of the Orinthian royal line
- (the) Valley- the ship of Sahar Bow, known for its dark green decks
- (the) Wilds- the northernmost country of the continent, closest to the Shadow Wall, groups of tribes who were defeated by Orinth years before in the War of the Wilds

About the Author

Summer Sullivan is a college student who grew up in rural Northern Michigan and attended a small high school. She enjoys biking, golfing, writing, and spending time with friends and family. Currently, Summer spends her time between her hometown and Northern Florida, writing as much as she can.

Made in the USA
Middletown, DE
20 October 2022